OUT OF THIN AIR

HÄGAR

THE HORRIBLE

by Dik Browne

TOR

A TOM DOHERTY ASSOCIATES BOOK

This is a work of fiction. All the characters and events portrayed in this book are fictional, and any resemblance to real people or incidents is purely coincidental.

HAGAR THE HORRIBLE: OUT ON A LIMB

First Tor printing: November 1986

A TOR Book

Published by Tom Doherty Associates, Inc.
49 West 24 Street
New York, N.Y. 10010

ISBN: 0-812-56790-0
CAN. ED.: 0-812-56791-9

Printed in the United States of America

0 9 8 7 6 5 4 3 2 1

ANCHORS AWAY

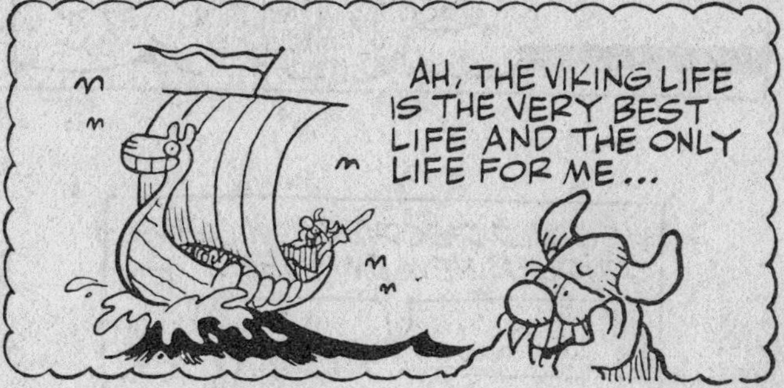
AH, THE VIKING LIFE IS THE VERY BEST LIFE AND THE ONLY LIFE FOR ME...

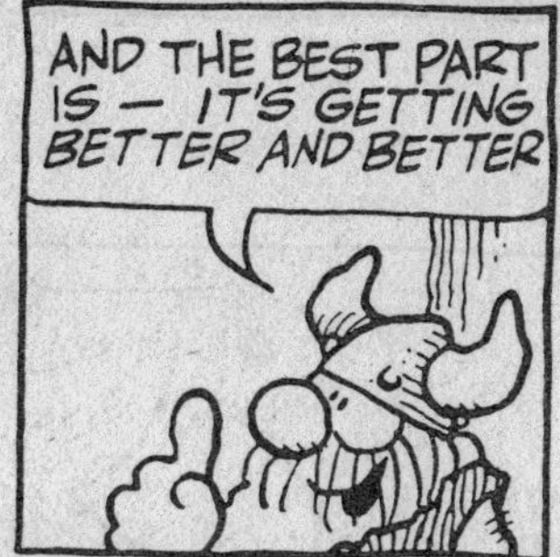
AND THE BEST PART IS — IT'S GETTING BETTER AND BETTER

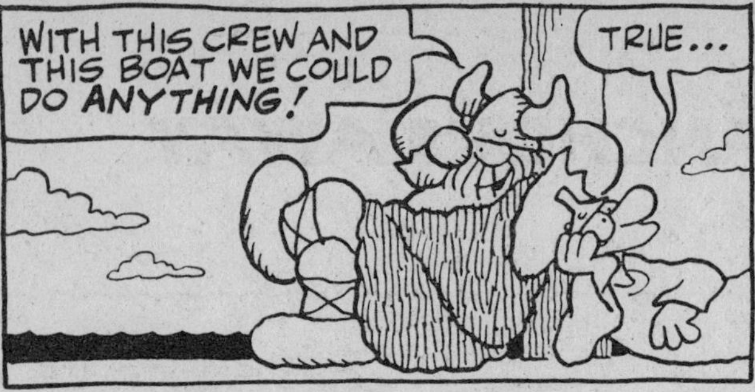
WITH THIS CREW AND THIS BOAT WE COULD DO ANYTHING!
TRUE...

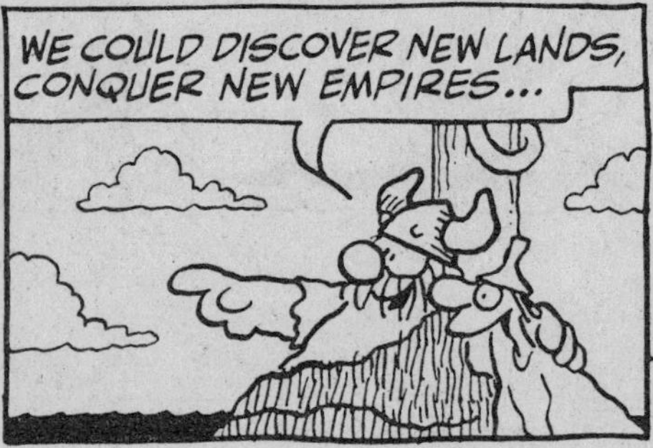
WE COULD DISCOVER NEW LANDS, CONQUER NEW EMPIRES...

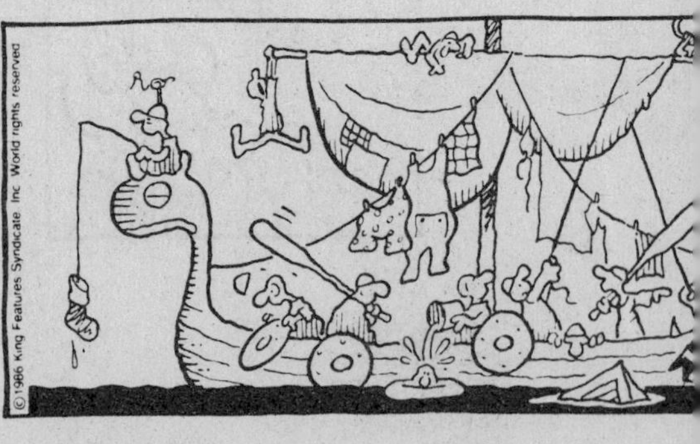

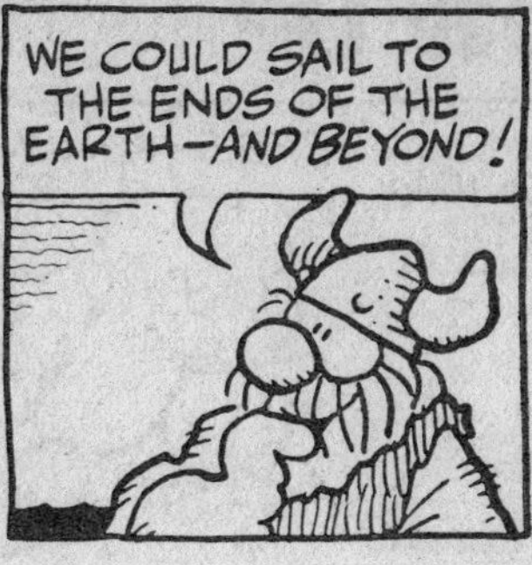
WE COULD SAIL TO THE ENDS OF THE EARTH—AND BEYOND!

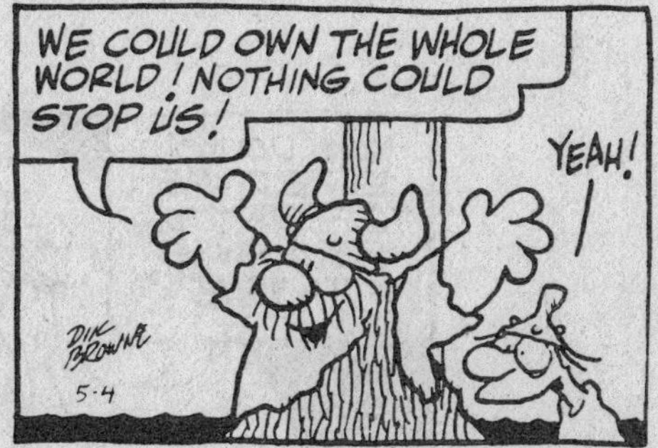
WE COULD OWN THE WHOLE WORLD! NOTHING COULD STOP US!
YEAH!
5-4

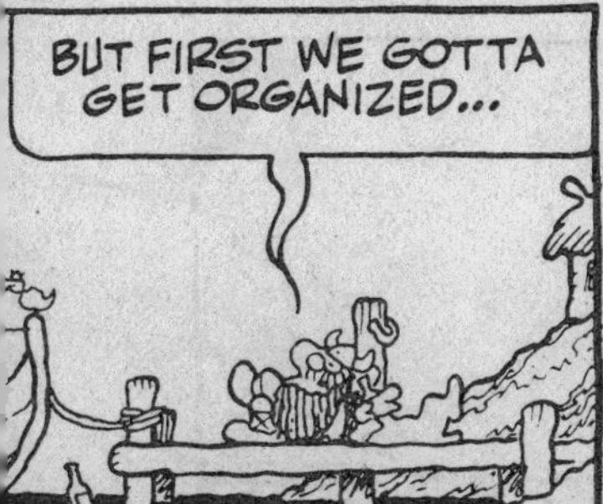
BUT FIRST WE GOTTA GET ORGANIZED...

BLOW UP

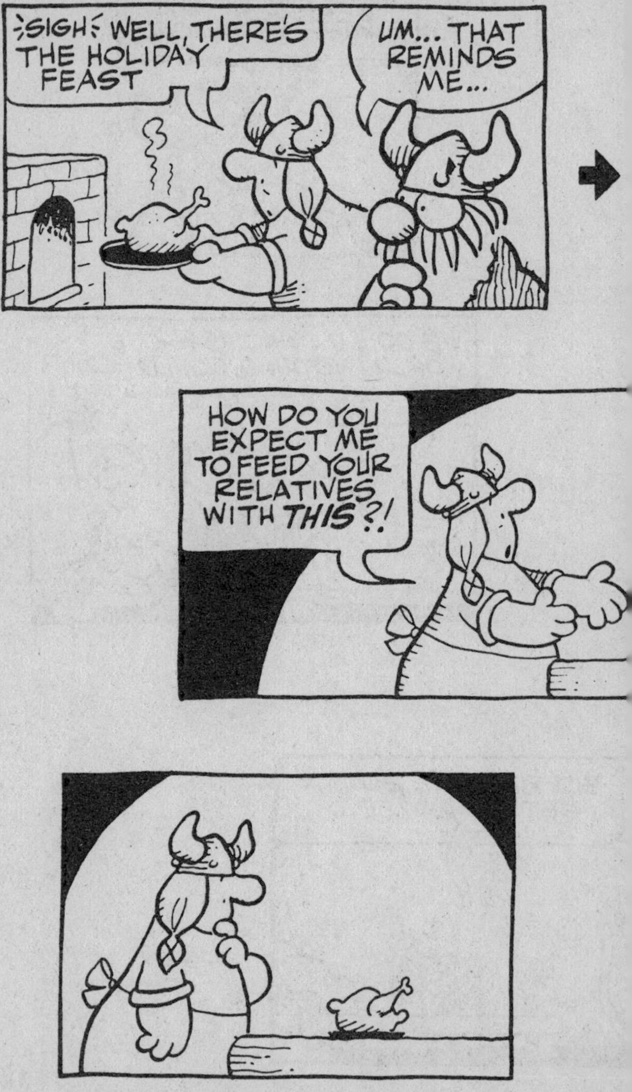

SIGH WELL, THERE'S THE HOLIDAY FEAST
UM... THAT REMINDS ME...
HOW DO YOU EXPECT ME TO FEED YOUR RELATIVES WITH *THIS*?!

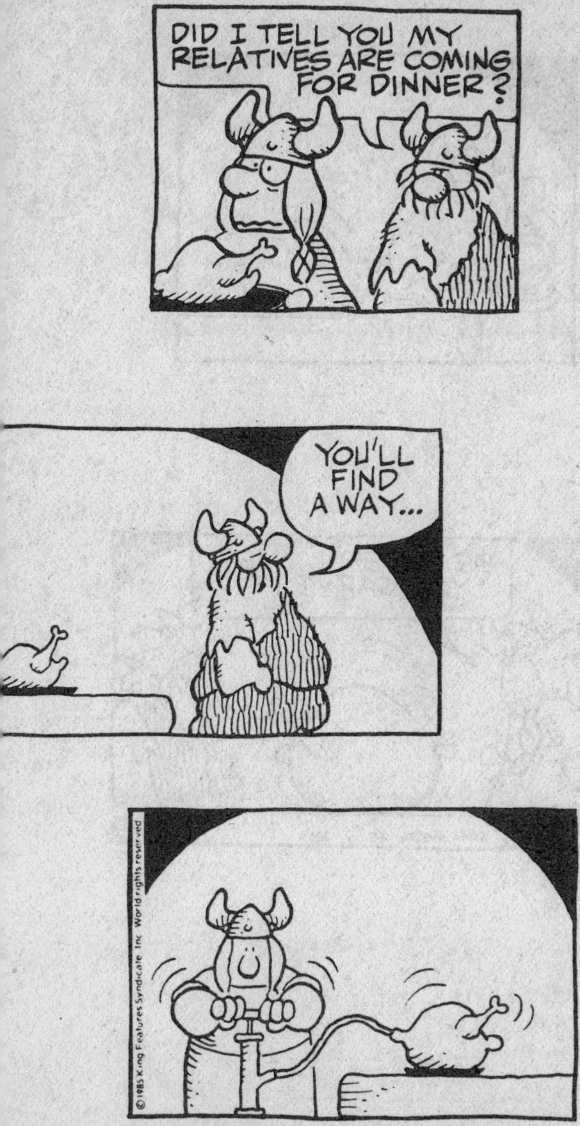
DID I TELL YOU MY RELATIVES ARE COMING FOR DINNER?
YOU'LL FIND A WAY...
© 1985 King Features Syndicate Inc World rights reserved

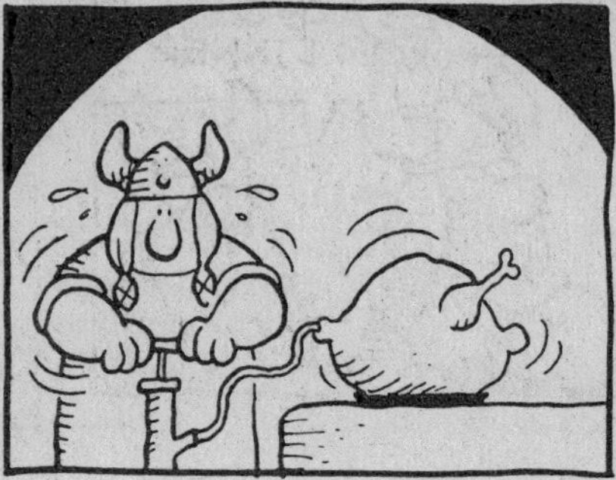

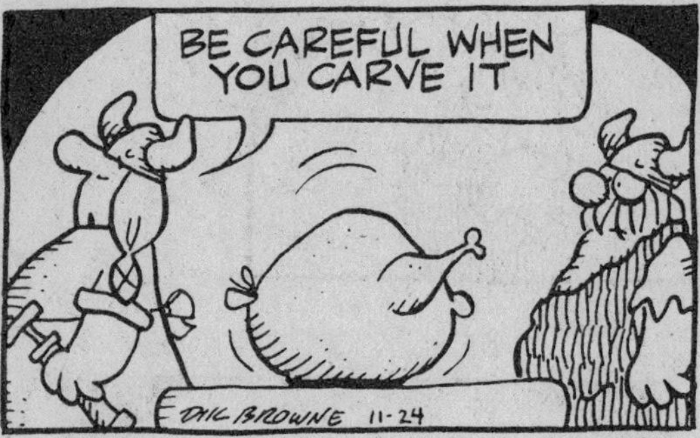
BE CAREFUL WHEN YOU CARVE IT
DIK BROWNE 11-24

HOLD ON

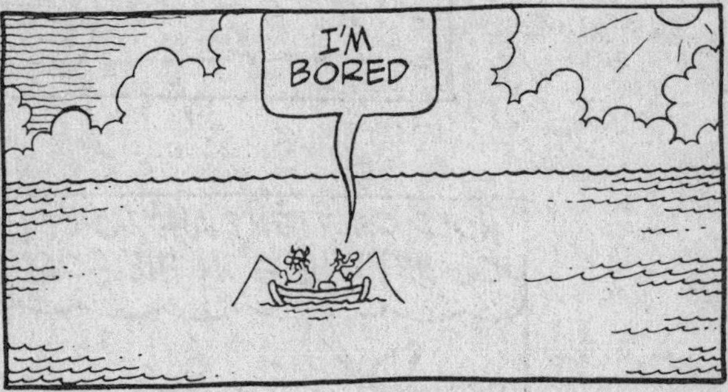
I'M BORED

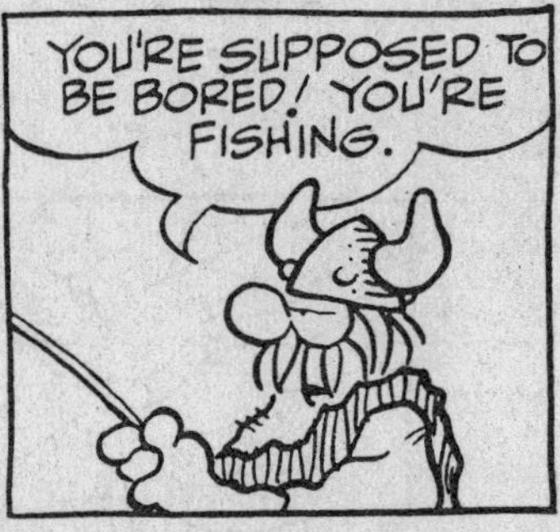
YOU'RE SUPPOSED TO BE BORED! YOU'RE FISHING.

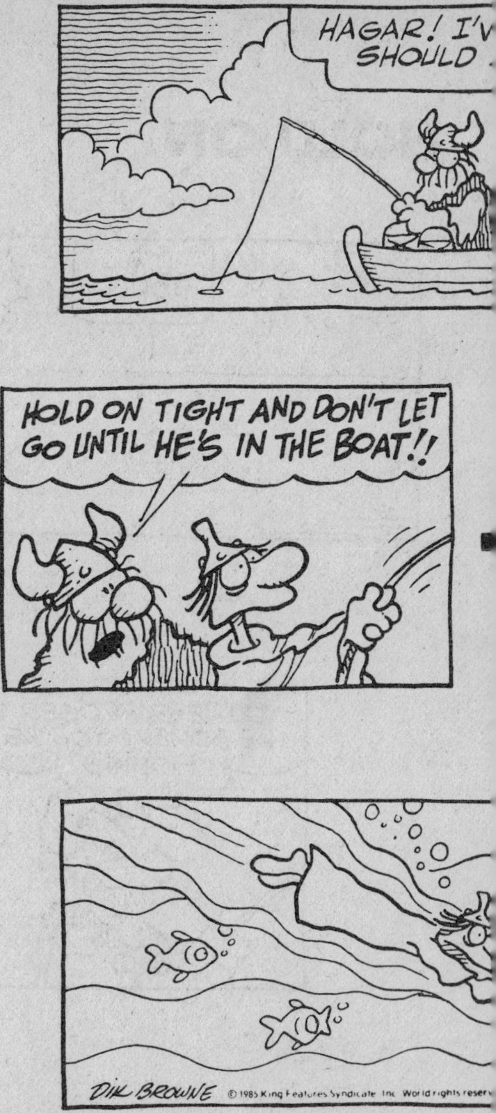
HAGAR!
SHOULD
HOLD ON TIGHT AND DON'T LET GO UNTIL HE'S IN THE BOAT!!
DIK BROWNE
© 1985 King Features Syndicate Inc World rights reserv

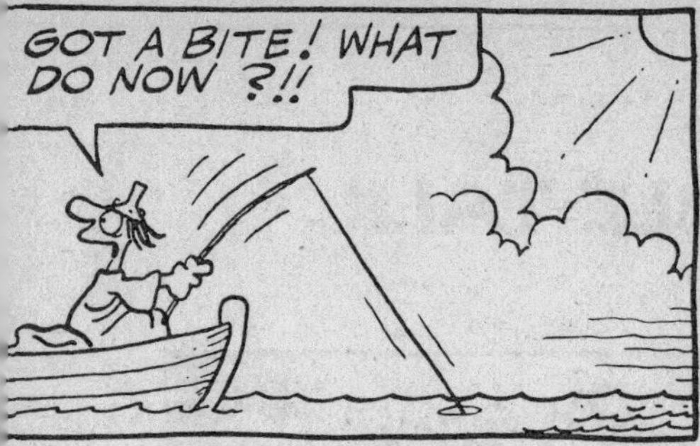
GOT A BITE! WHAT DO NOW ?!!

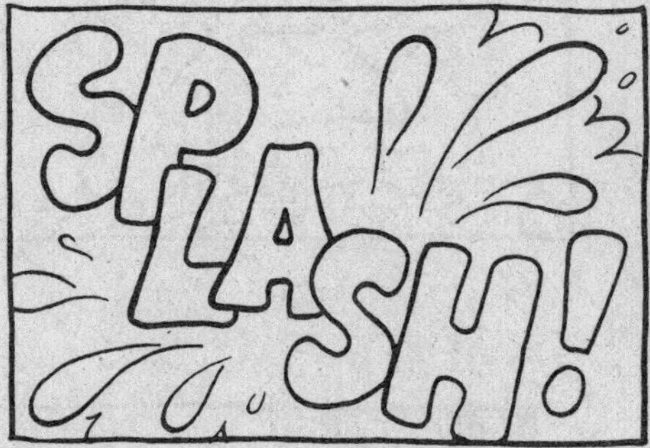
SPLASH!

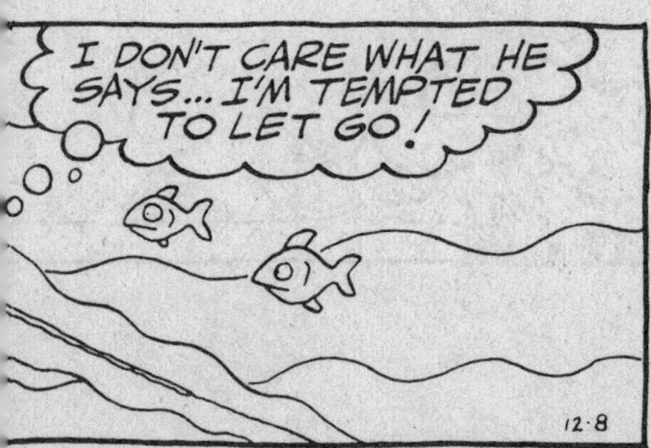
I DON'T CARE WHAT HE SAYS... I'M TEMPTED TO LET GO!
12·8

TABLE TALK

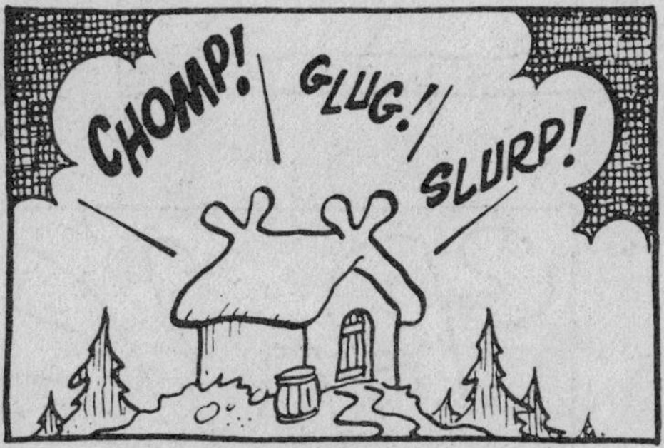
CHOMP!
GLUG.!
SLURP!

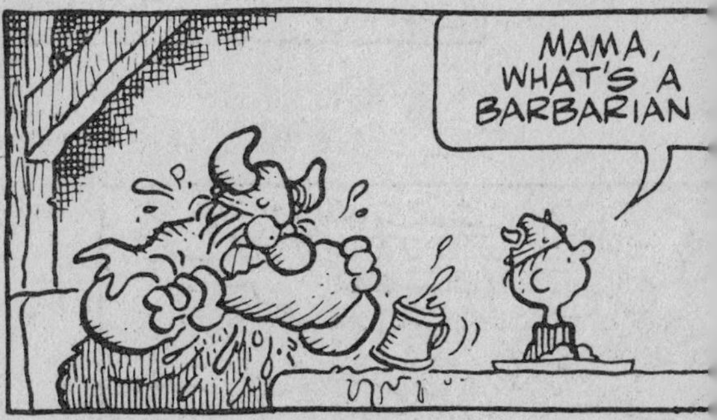
MAMA, WHAT'S A BARBARIAN

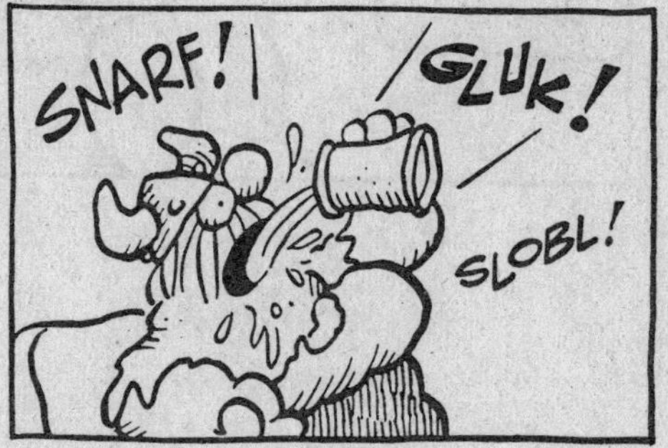
SNARF!
GLUK!
SLOBL!

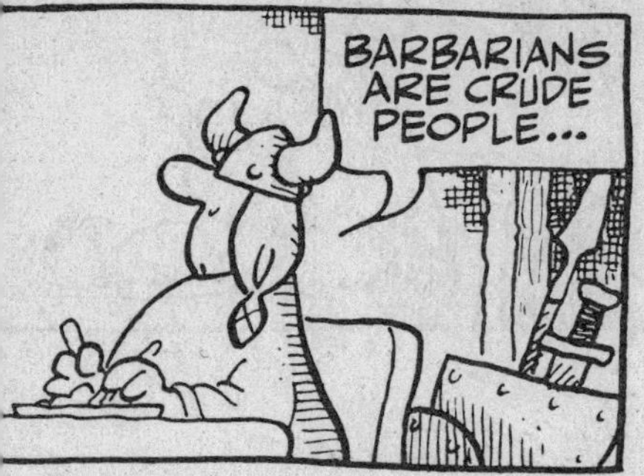
BARBARIANS ARE CRUDE PEOPLE...

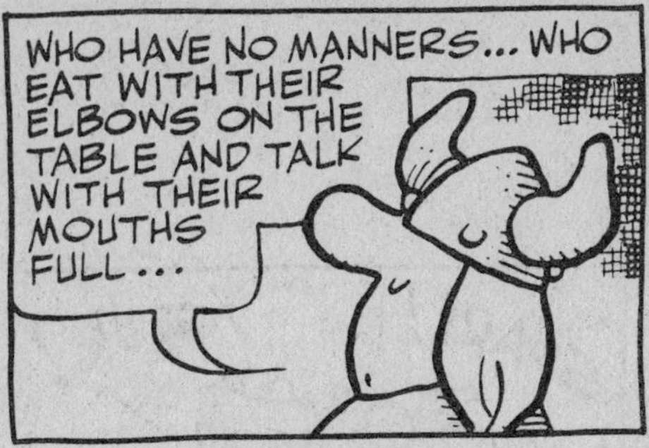
WHO HAVE NO MANNERS... WHO EAT WITH THEIR ELBOWS ON THE TABLE AND TALK WITH THEIR MOUTHS FULL...

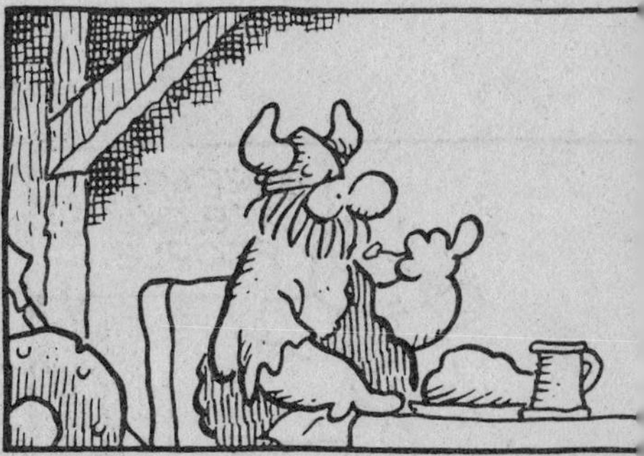

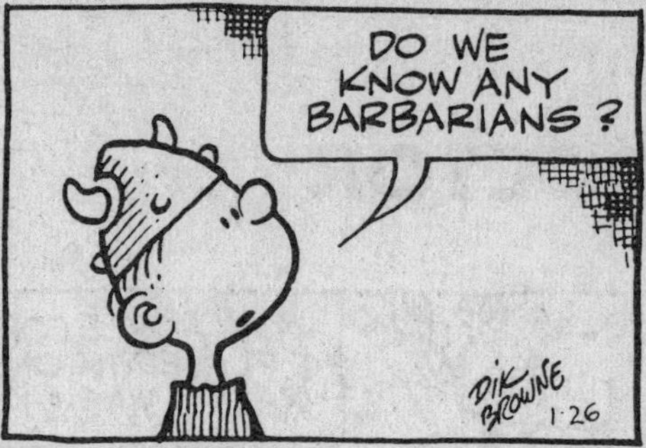
DO WE KNOW ANY BARBARIANS ?
DIK BROWNE 1·26

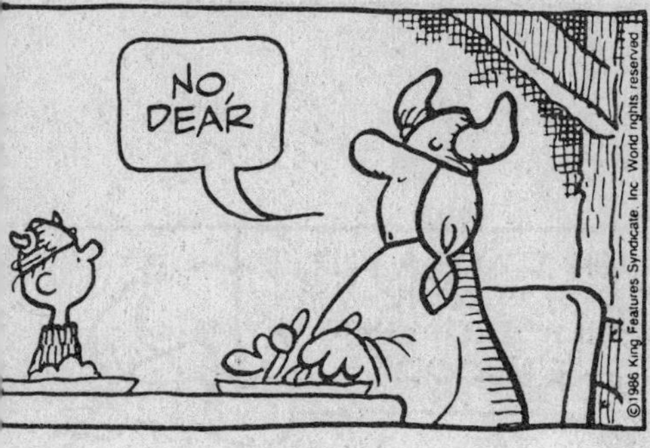
NO, DEAR
©1986 King Features Syndicate, Inc. World rights reserved

DOCTOR

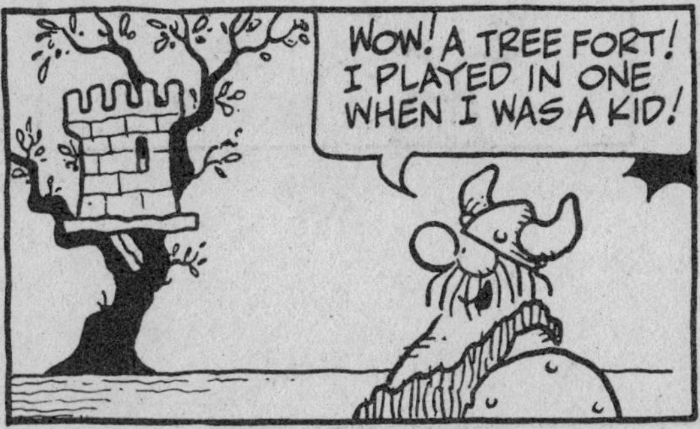
WOW! A TREE FORT! I PLAYED IN ONE WHEN I WAS A KID!

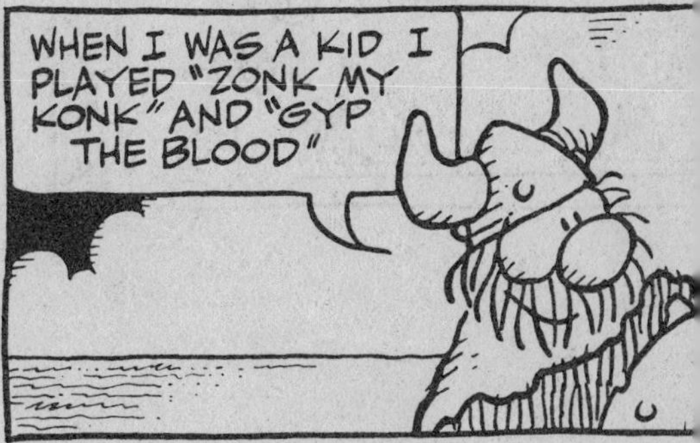
WHEN I WAS A KID I PLAYED "ZONK MY KONK" AND "GYP THE BLOOD"

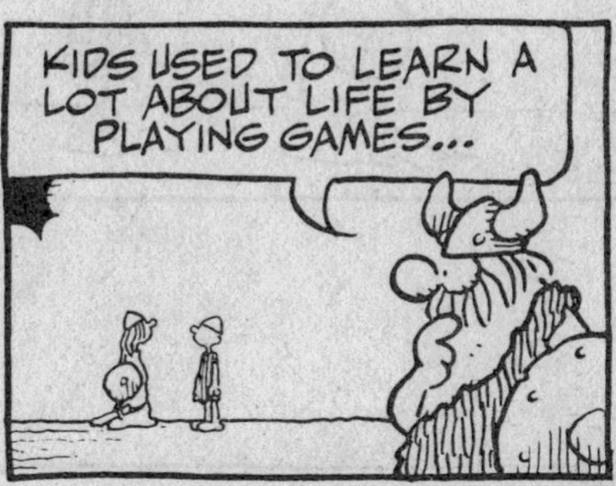
KIDS USED TO LEARN A LOT ABOUT LIFE BY PLAYING GAMES...

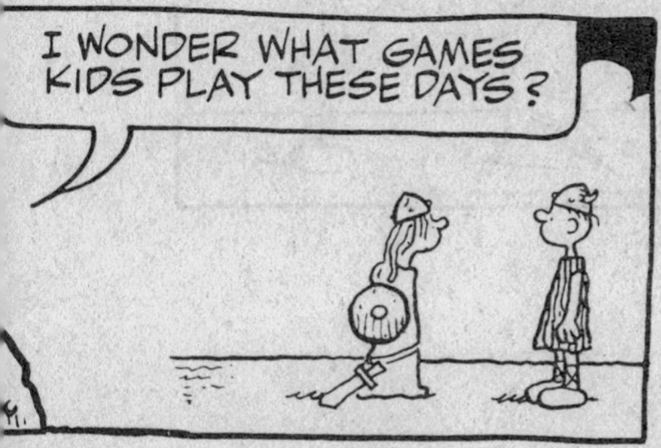
I WONDER WHAT GAMES KIDS PLAY THESE DAYS?

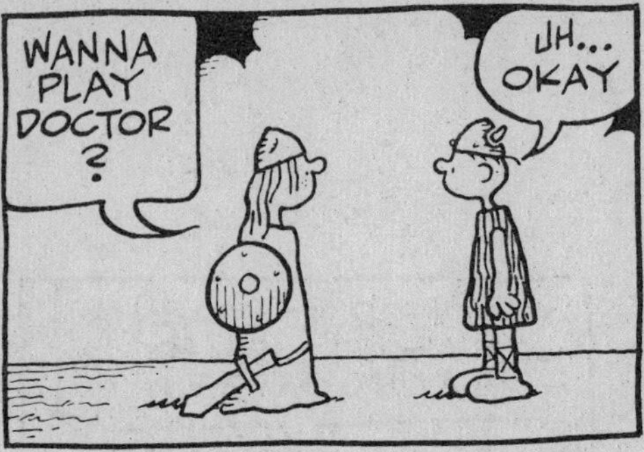
WANNA PLAY DOCTOR ?
UH... OKAY

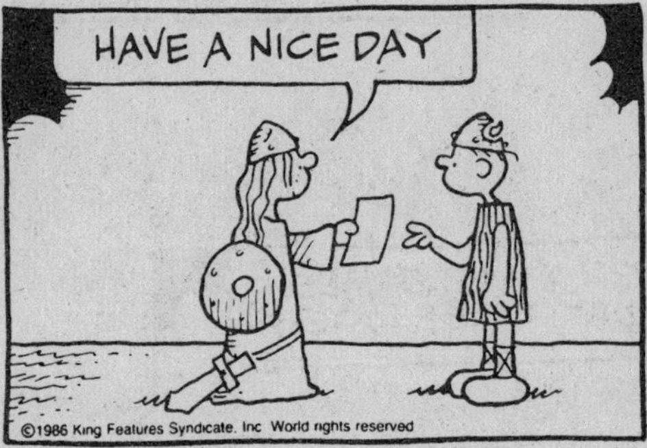
HAVE A NICE DAY
©1986 King Features Syndicate, Inc World rights reserved

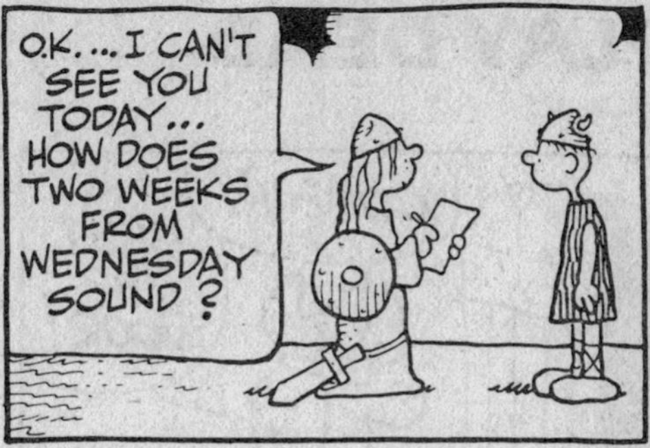
O.K. ... I CAN'T SEE YOU TODAY... HOW DOES TWO WEEKS FROM WEDNESDAY SOUND ?

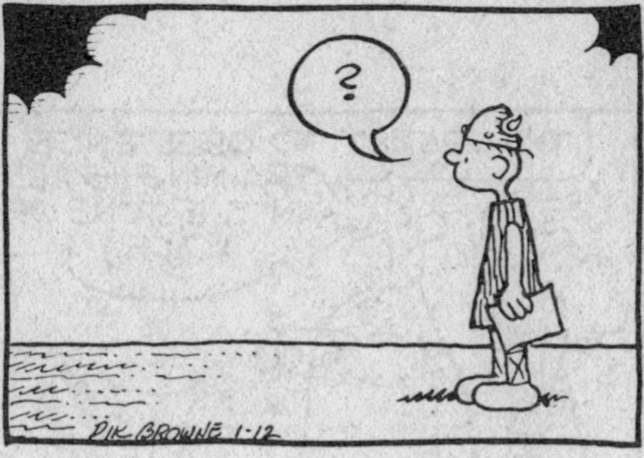
?
DIK BROWNE 1-12

PLAY DEAD

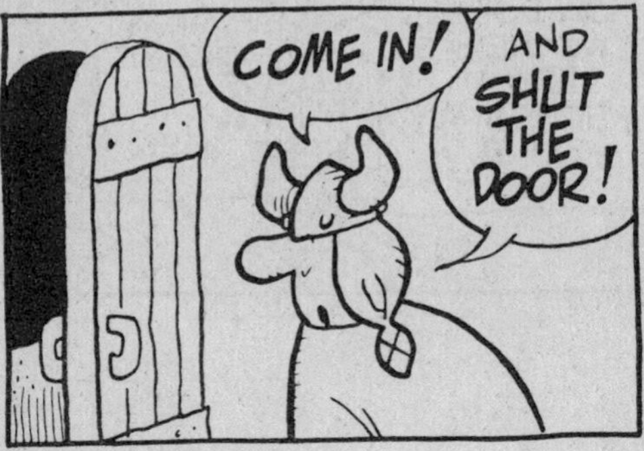
COME IN!
AND SHUT THE DOOR!

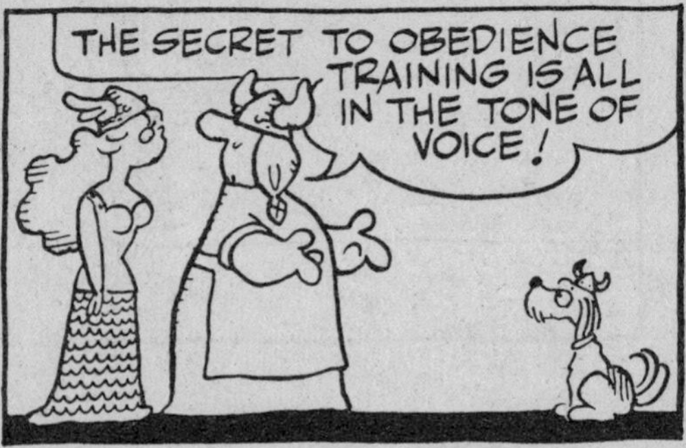
THE SECRET TO OBEDIENCE TRAINING IS ALL IN THE TONE OF VOICE!

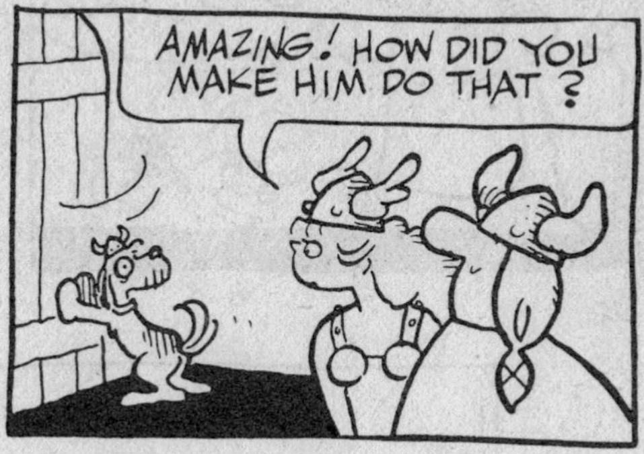
AMAZING! HOW DID YOU MAKE HIM DO THAT?

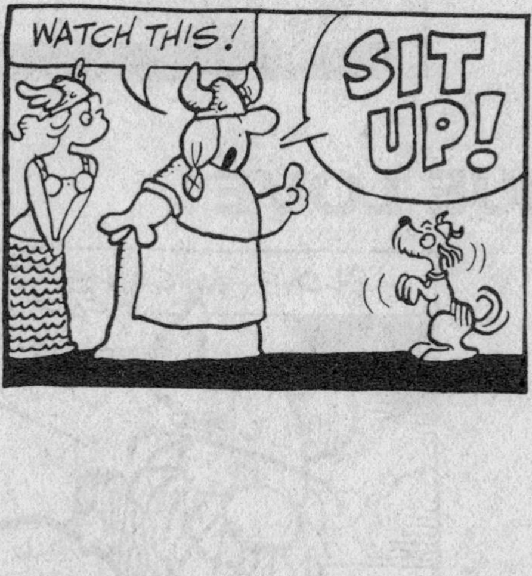
WATCH THIS!
SIT UP!

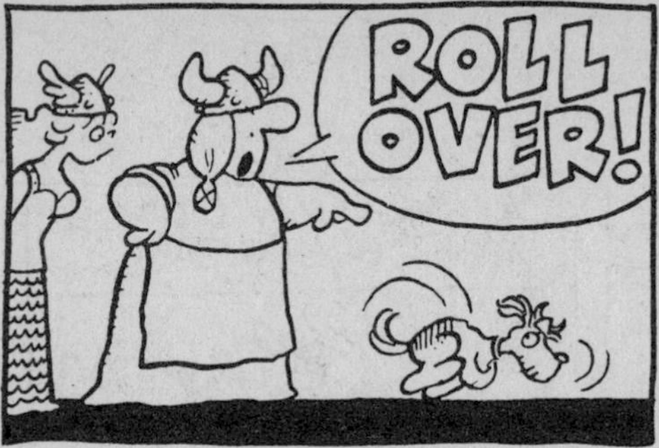
ROLL OVER!

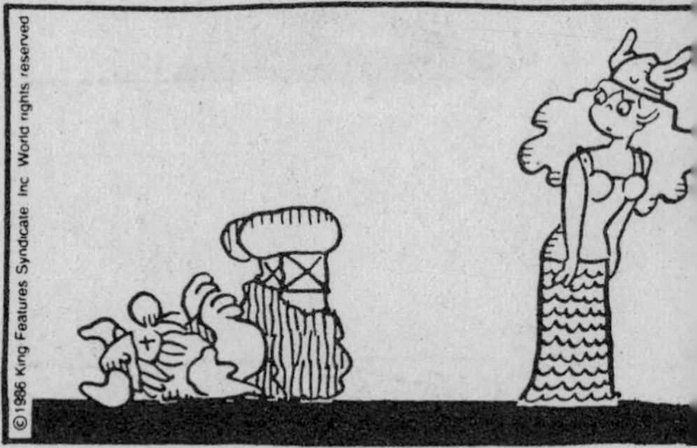
©1986 King Features Syndicate, Inc. World rights reserved

TRUE LOVE

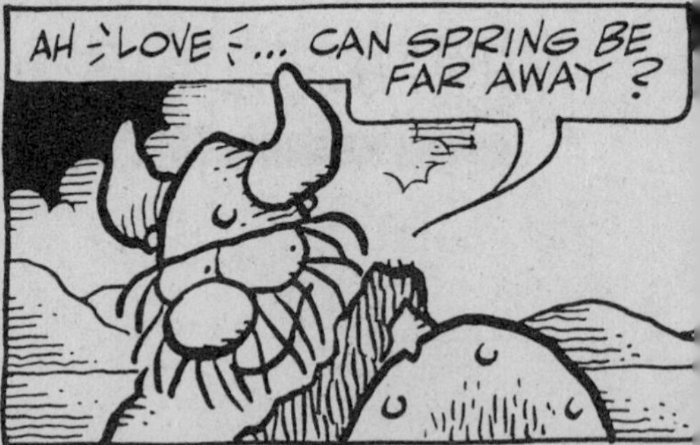
AH ~ LOVE ~ ... CAN SPRING BE FAR AWAY ?

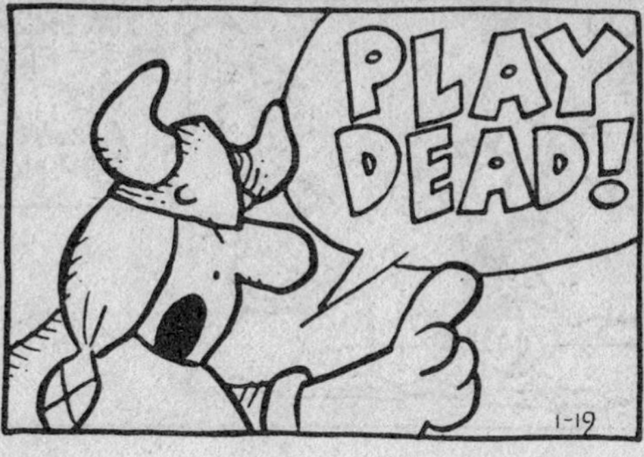
PLAY DEAD!
1-19

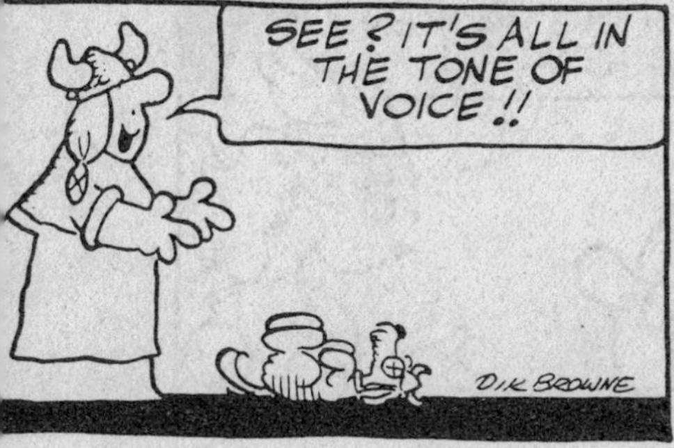
SEE ? IT'S ALL IN THE TONE OF VOICE !!
DIK BROWNE

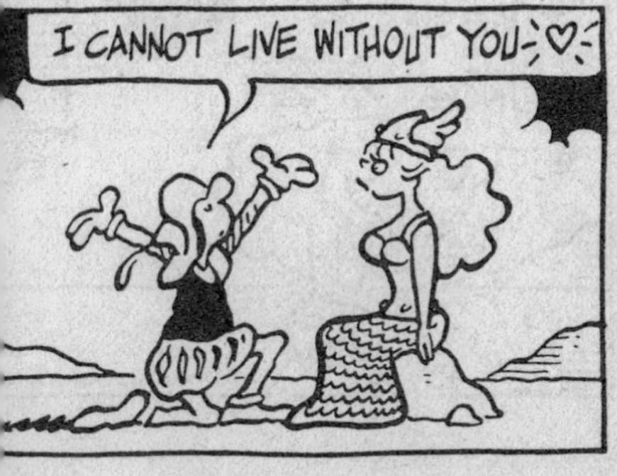
I CANNOT LIVE WITHOUT YOU

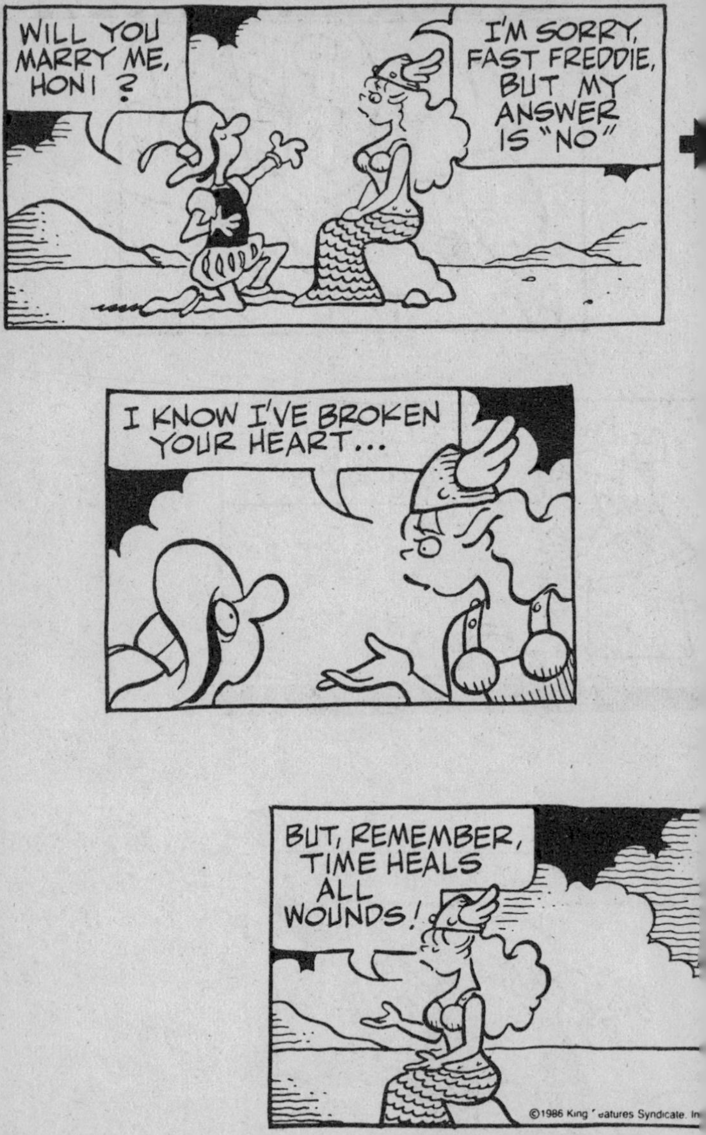
WILL YOU MARRY ME, HONI ?
I'M SORRY, FAST FREDDIE, BUT MY ANSWER IS "NO"
I KNOW I'VE BROKEN YOUR HEART...
BUT, REMEMBER, TIME HEALS ALL WOUNDS!
©1986 King 'eatures Syndicate. In

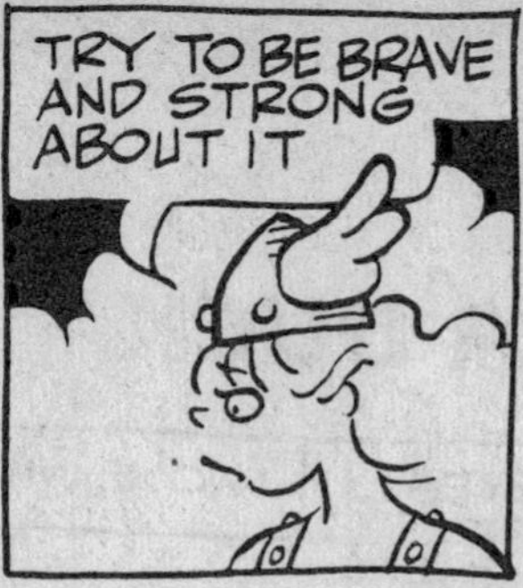
TRY TO BE BRAVE AND STRONG ABOUT IT

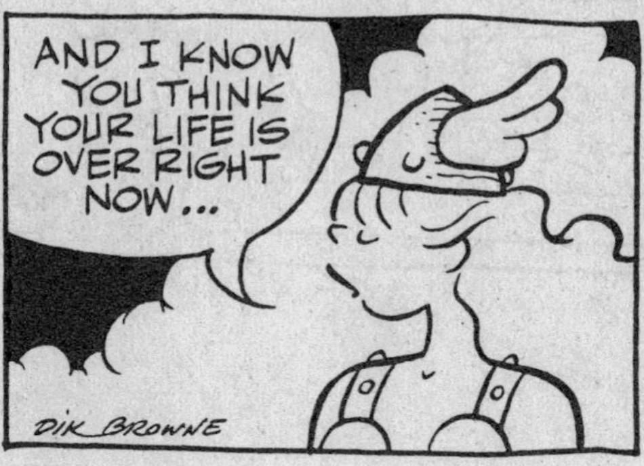
AND I KNOW YOU THINK YOUR LIFE IS OVER RIGHT NOW...
DIK BROWNE

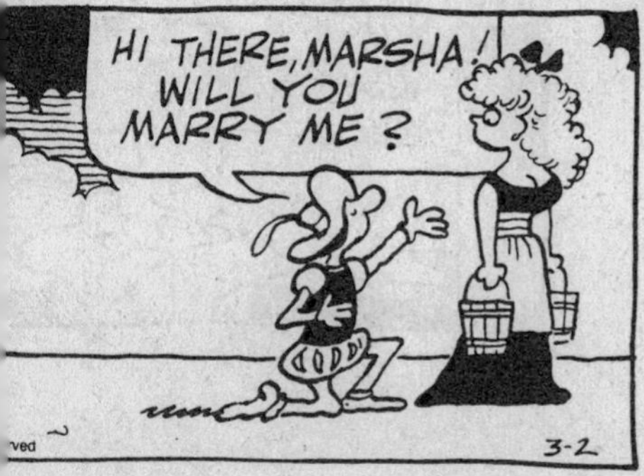
HI THERE, MARSHA! WILL YOU MARRY ME ?
rved
3-2

LOVE A DUCK

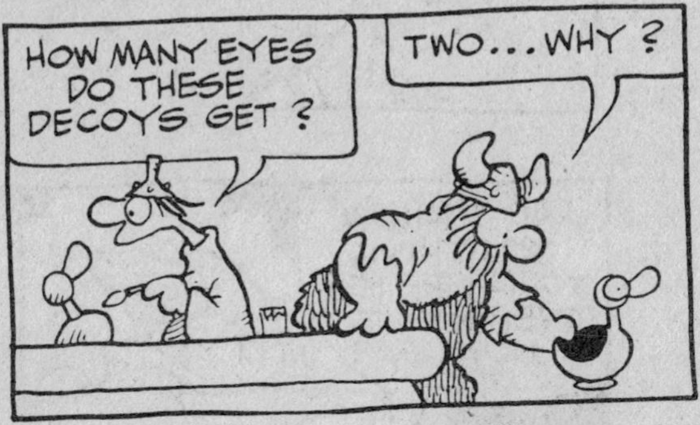
HOW MANY EYES DO THESE DECOYS GET ?
TWO...WHY ?

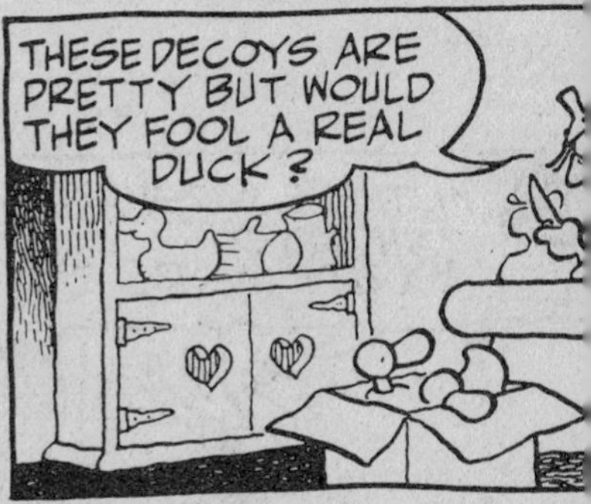
THESE DECOYS ARE PRETTY BUT WOULD THEY FOOL A REAL DUCK ?

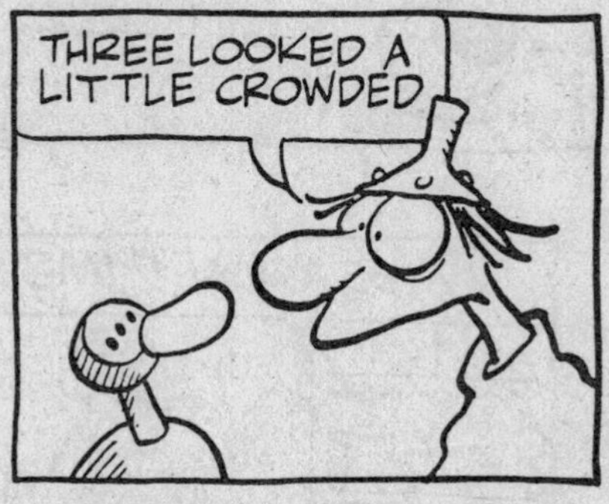
THREE LOOKED A LITTLE CROWDED

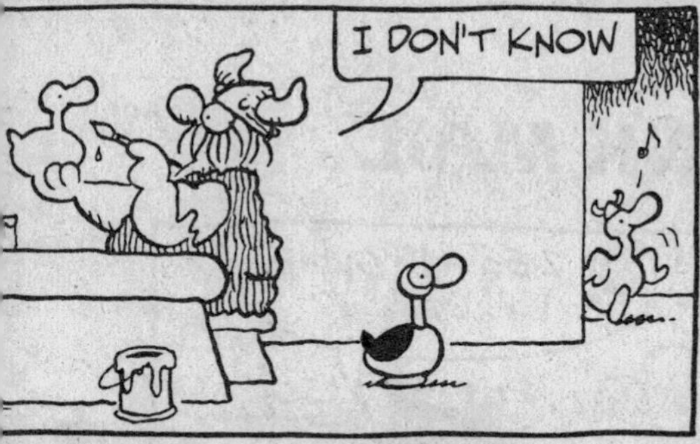
I DON'T KNOW

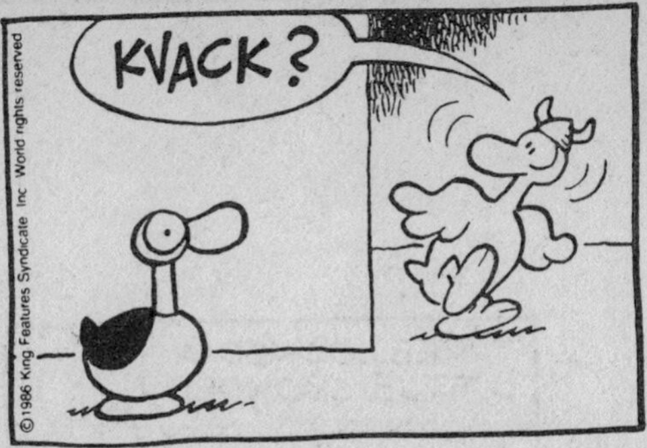
KVACK?
©1986 King Features Syndicate Inc World rights reserved

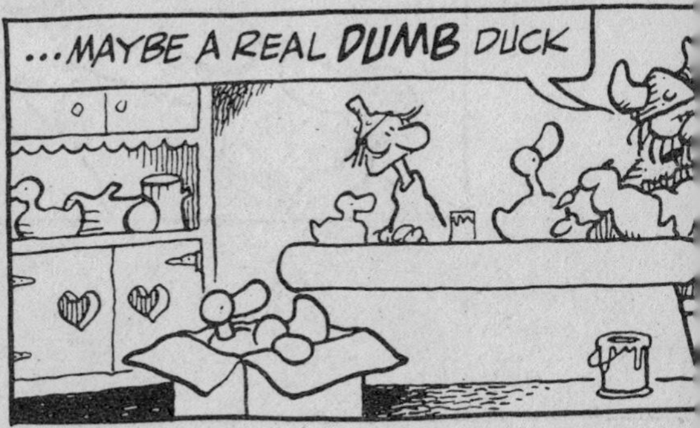
...MAYBE A REAL DUMB DUCK

JUNK MAIL

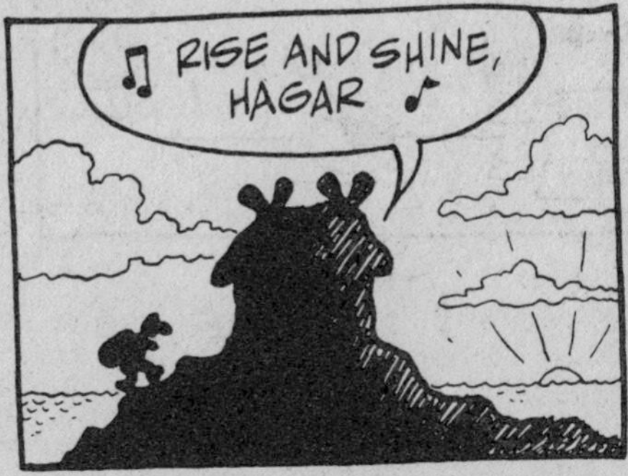
RISE AND SHINE, HAGAR

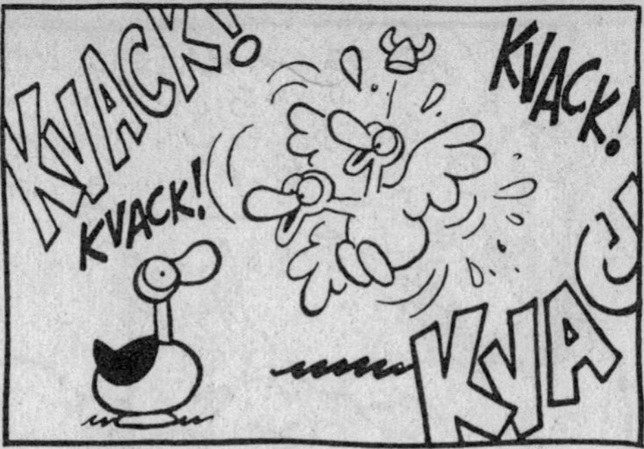
KVACK!
KVACK!
KVACK!
KVAC

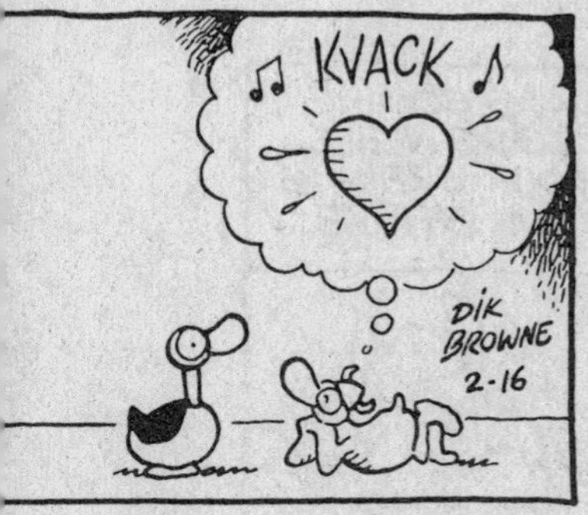
KVACK
DIK BROWNE 2-16

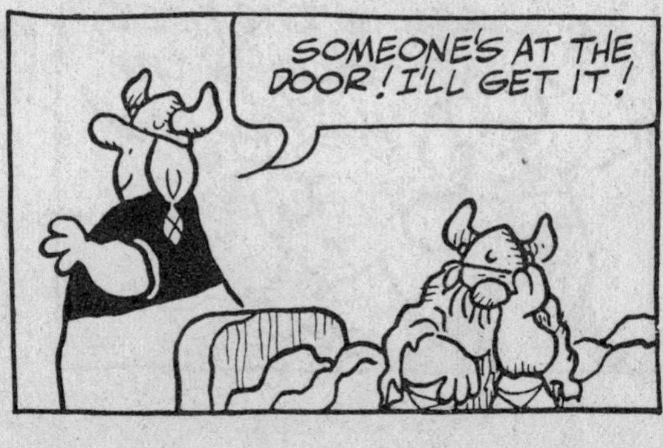
SOMEONE'S AT THE DOOR! I'LL GET IT!

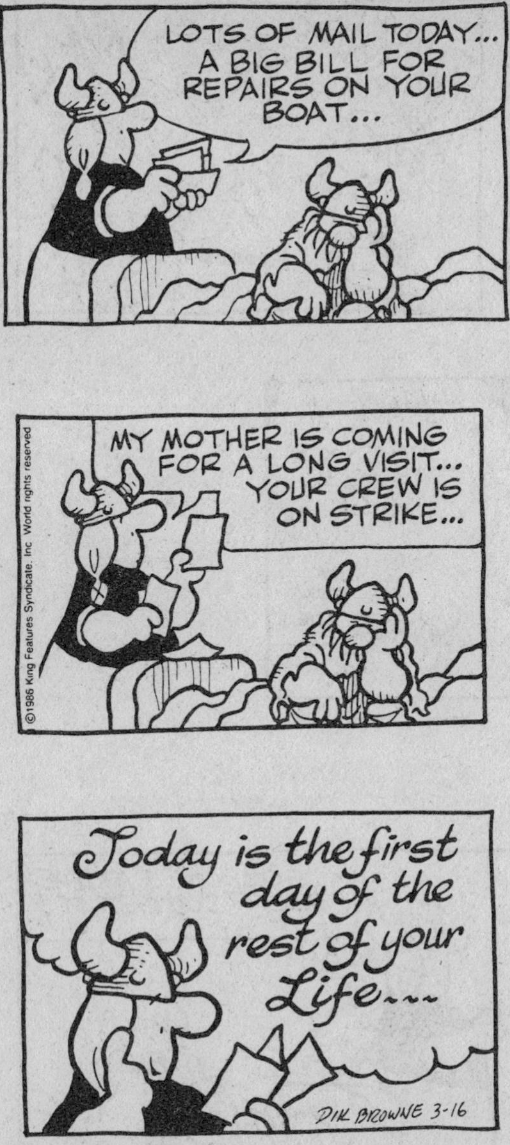
LOTS OF MAIL TODAY... A BIG BILL FOR REPAIRS ON YOUR BOAT...
MY MOTHER IS COMING FOR A LONG VISIT... YOUR CREW IS ON STRIKE...
Today is the first day of the rest of your Life...
DIK BROWNE 3-16

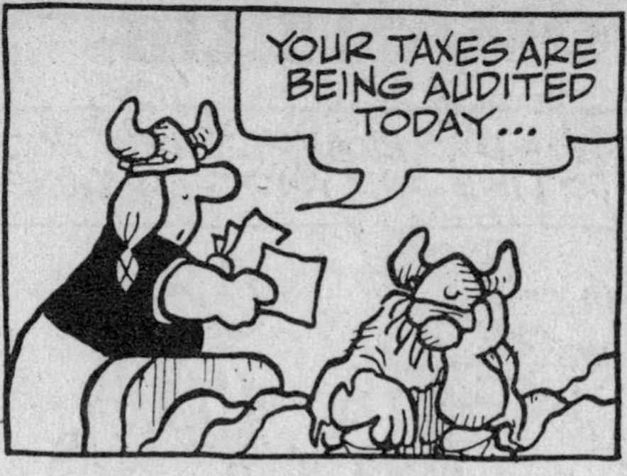
YOUR TAXES ARE BEING AUDITED TODAY...

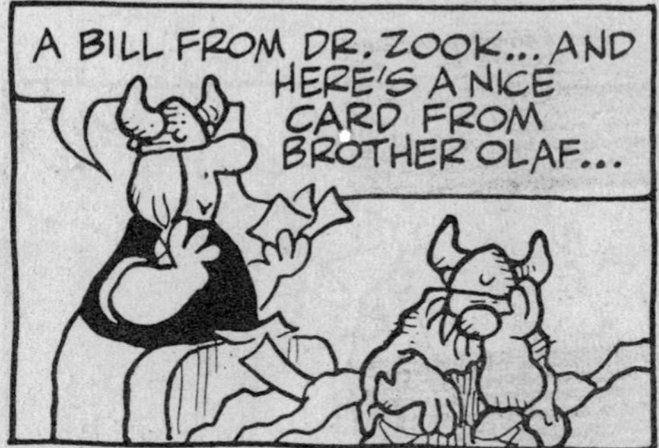
A BILL FROM DR. ZOOK... AND HERE'S A NICE CARD FROM BROTHER OLAF...

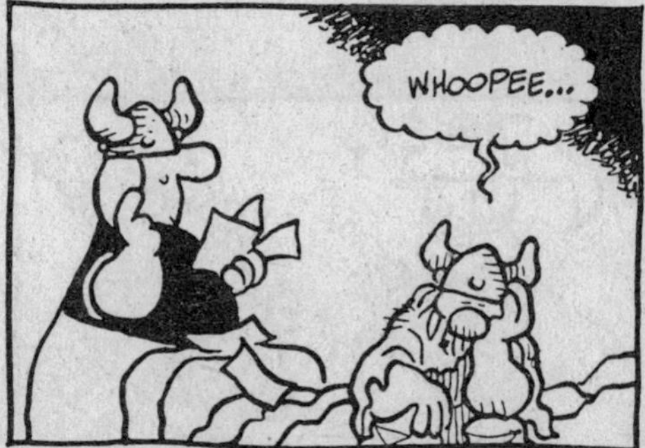
WHOOPEE...

WOMAN'S LIB

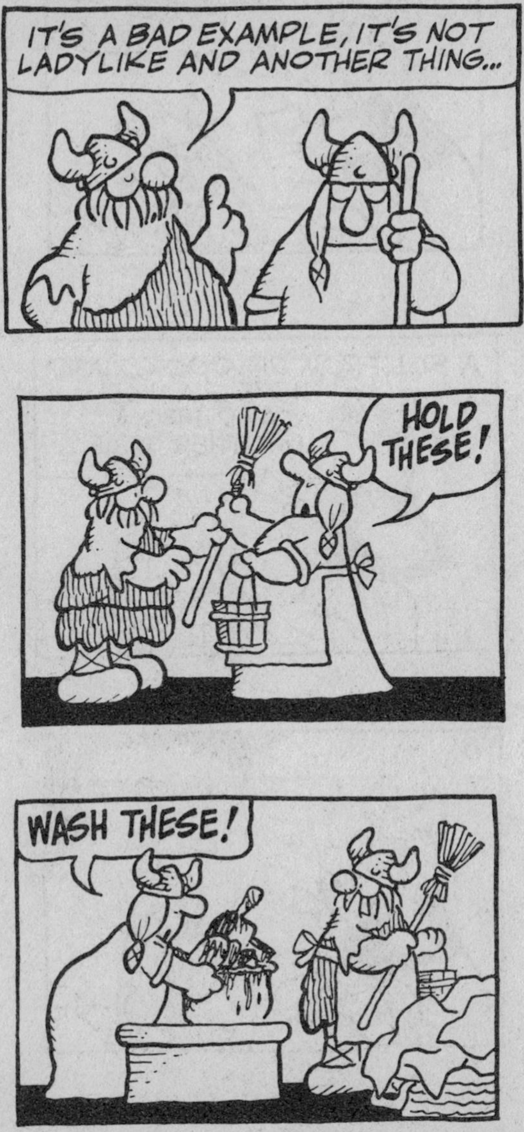
IT'S A BAD EXAMPLE, IT'S NOT LADYLIKE AND ANOTHER THING...
HOLD THESE!
WASH THESE!

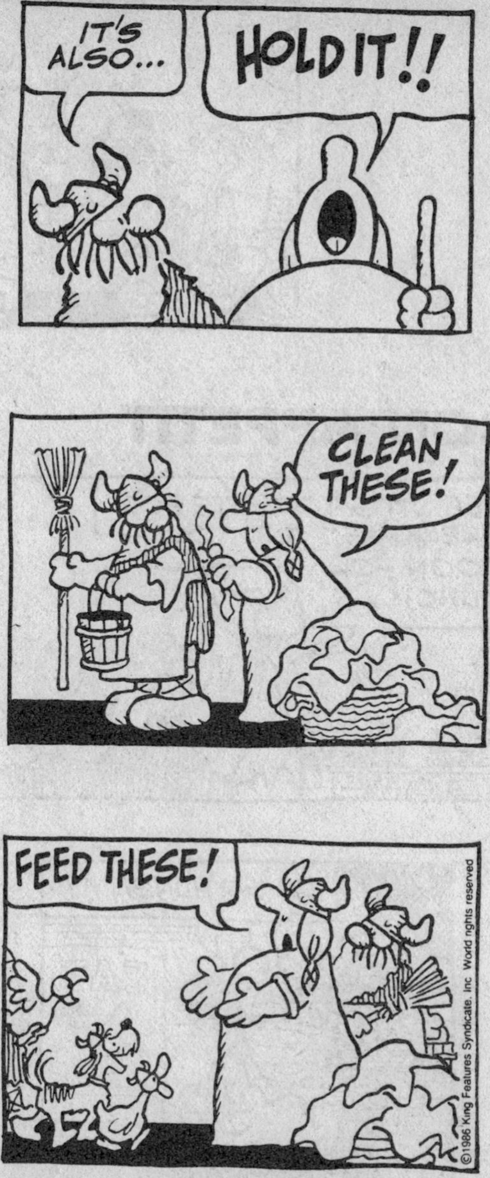
IT'S ALSO...
HOLD IT!!
CLEAN THESE!
FEED THESE!

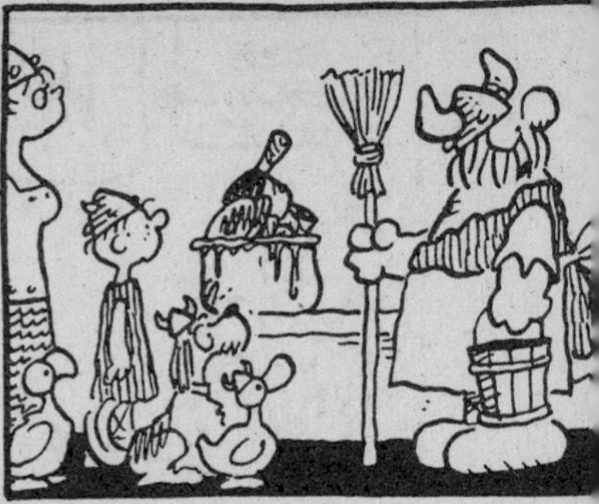

BON APPETIT

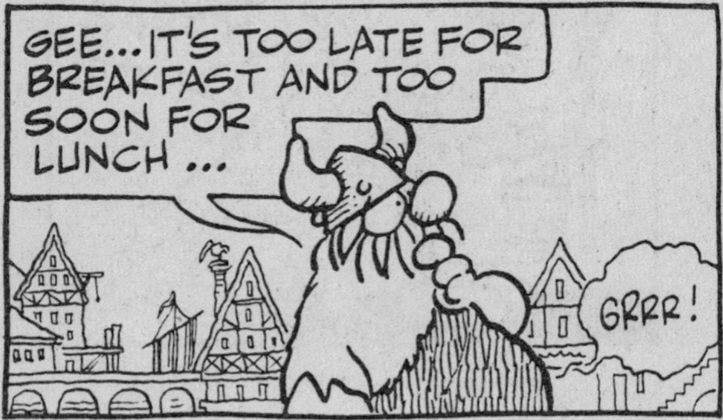
GEE...IT'S TOO LATE FOR BREAKFAST AND TOO SOON FOR LUNCH ...
GRRR!

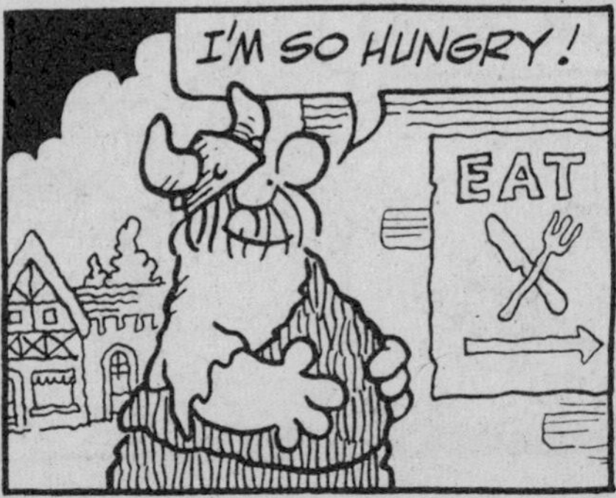
I'M SO HUNGRY!
EAT

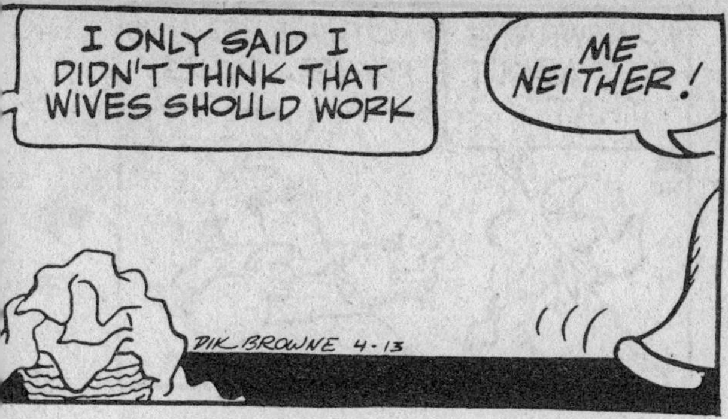
I ONLY SAID I DIDN'T THINK THAT WIVES SHOULD WORK
ME NEITHER!
DIK BROWNE 4-13

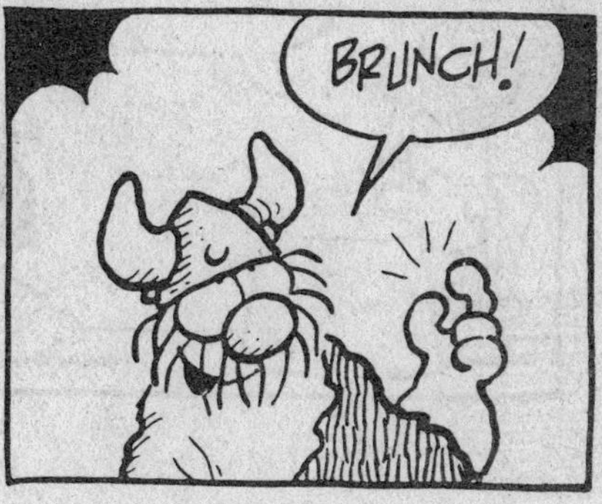
BRUNCH!

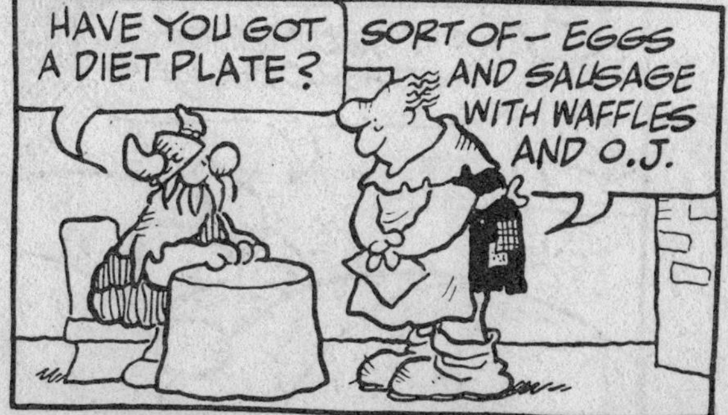
HAVE YOU GOT A DIET PLATE?
SORT OF - EGGS AND SAUSAGE WITH WAFFLES AND O.J.

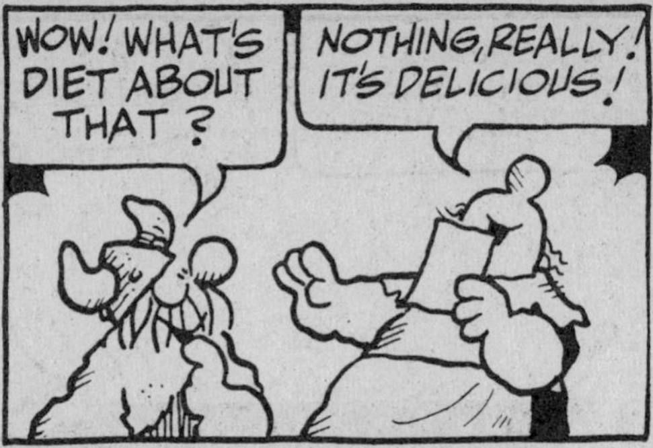
WOW! WHAT'S DIET ABOUT THAT?
NOTHING, REALLY! IT'S DELICIOUS!

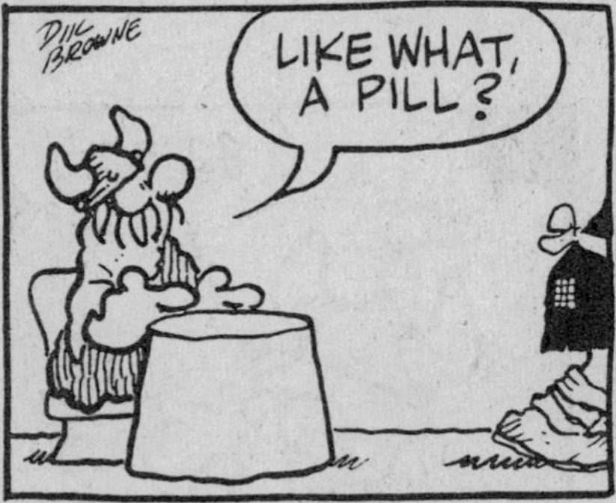
DIK BROWNE
LIKE WHAT, A PILL?

BACK TO BED

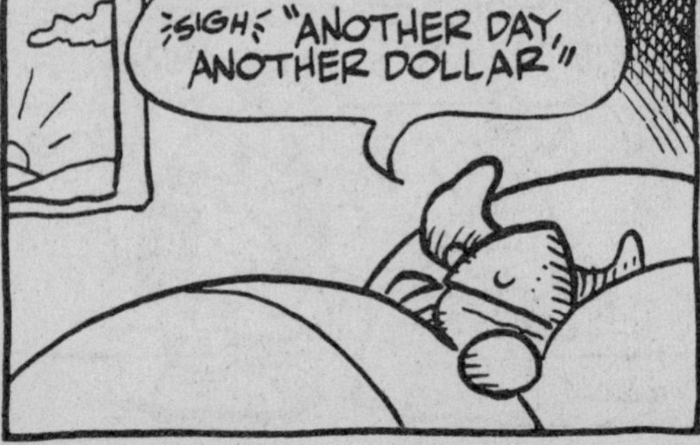
SIGH "ANOTHER DAY, ANOTHER DOLLAR"

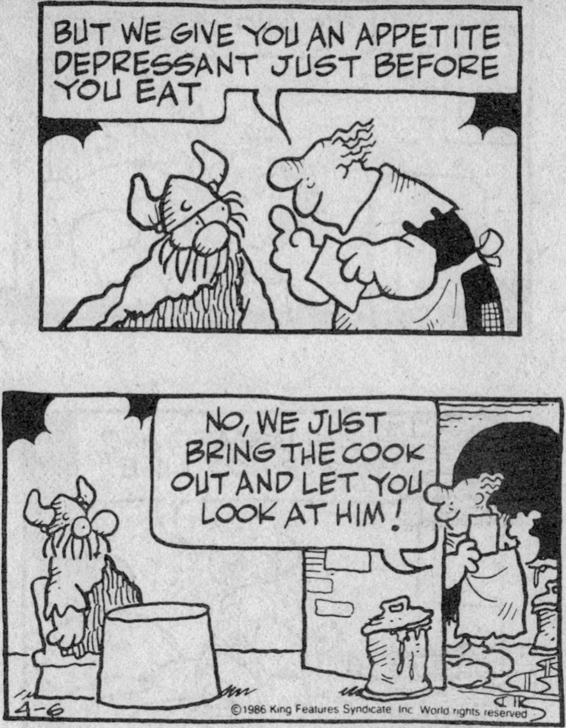
BUT WE GIVE YOU AN APPETITE DEPRESSANT JUST BEFORE YOU EAT
NO, WE JUST BRING THE COOK OUT AND LET YOU LOOK AT HIM!
4-6
©1986 King Features Syndicate Inc World rights reserved

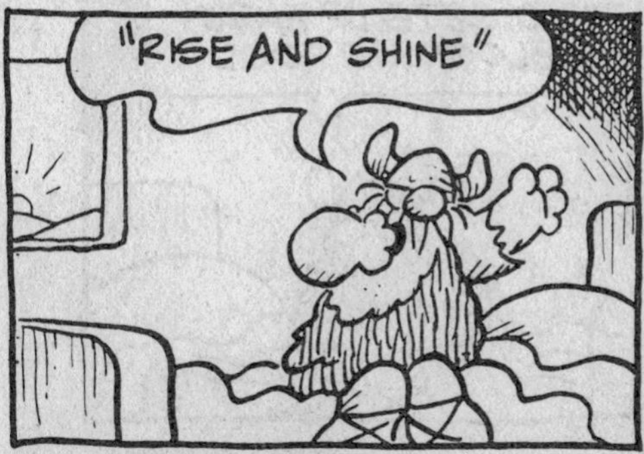
"RISE AND SHINE"

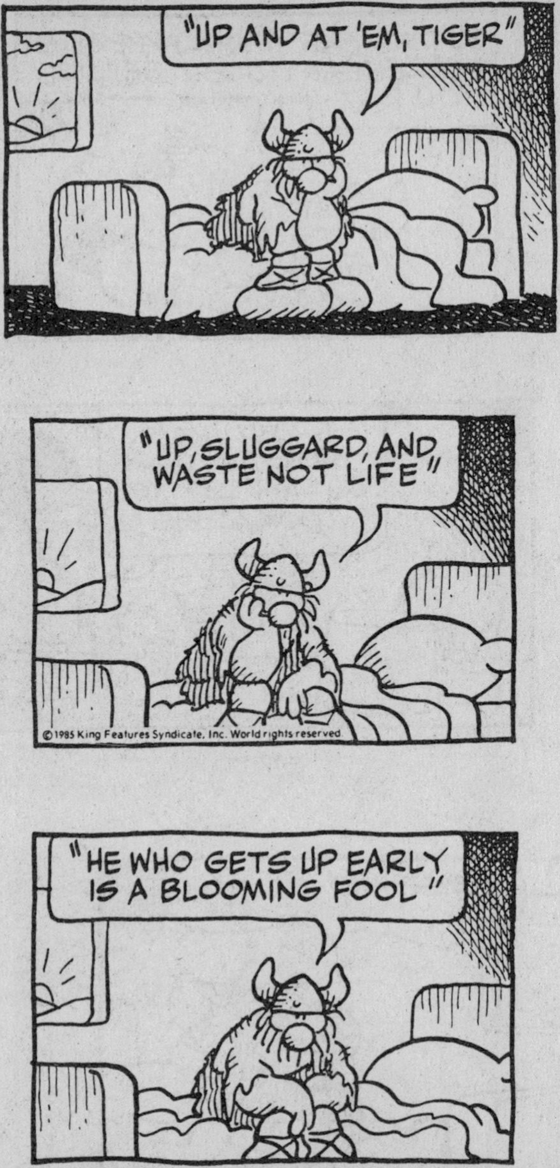
"UP AND AT 'EM, TIGER"
"UP, SLUGGARD, AND WASTE NOT LIFE"
© 1985 King Features Syndicate, Inc. World rights reserved.
"HE WHO GETS UP EARLY IS A BLOOMING FOOL"

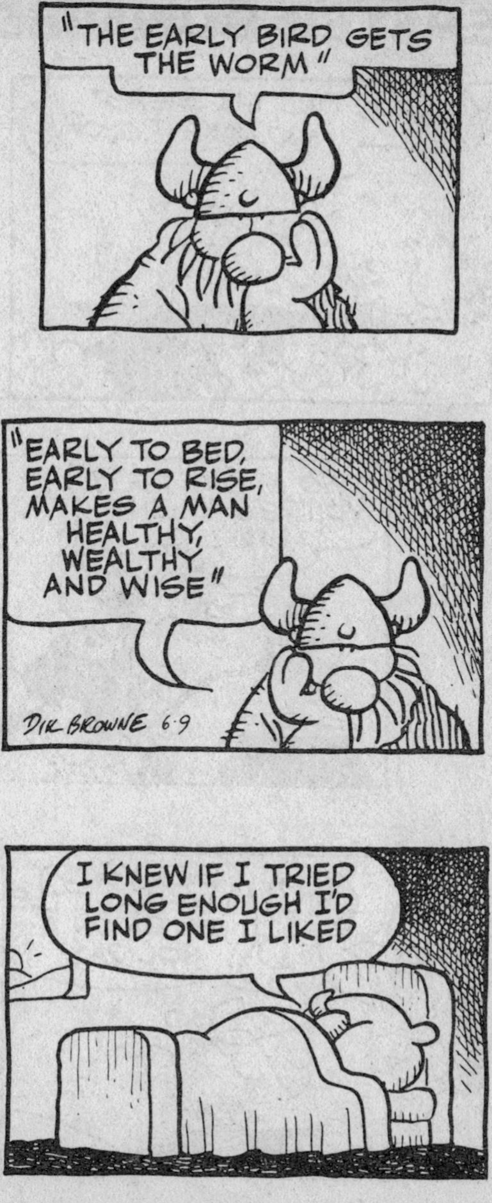
"THE EARLY BIRD GETS THE WORM"
"EARLY TO BED, EARLY TO RISE, MAKES A MAN HEALTHY, WEALTHY AND WISE"
DIK BROWNE 6·9
I KNEW IF I TRIED LONG ENOUGH I'D FIND ONE I LIKED

EASTER BUNNIES

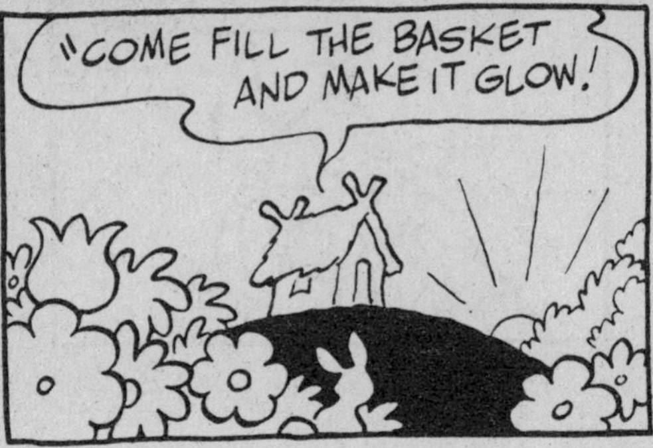
"COME FILL THE BASKET AND MAKE IT GLOW!

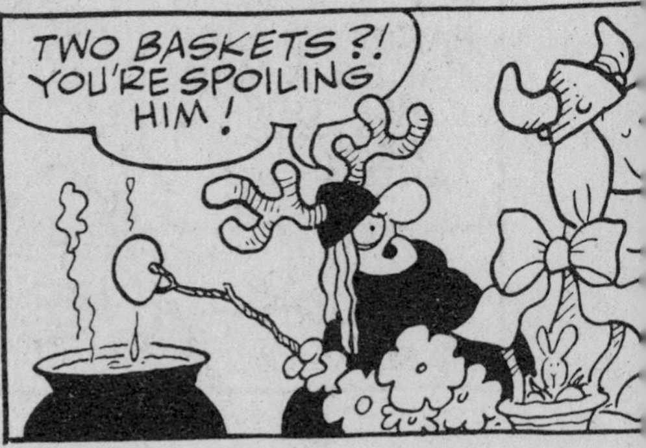
TWO BASKETS?! YOU'RE SPOILING HIM!

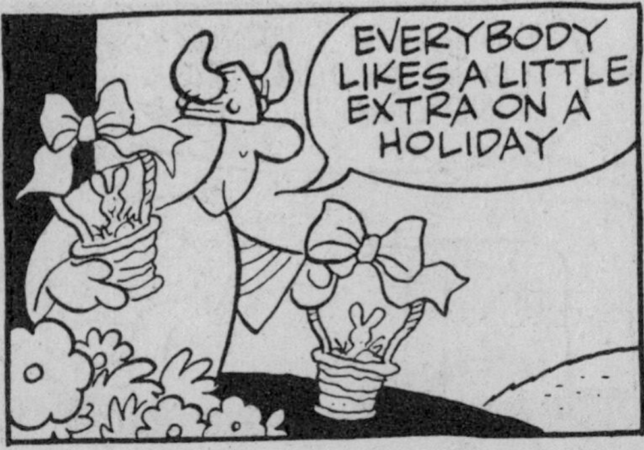
EVERYBODY LIKES A LITTLE EXTRA ON A HOLIDAY

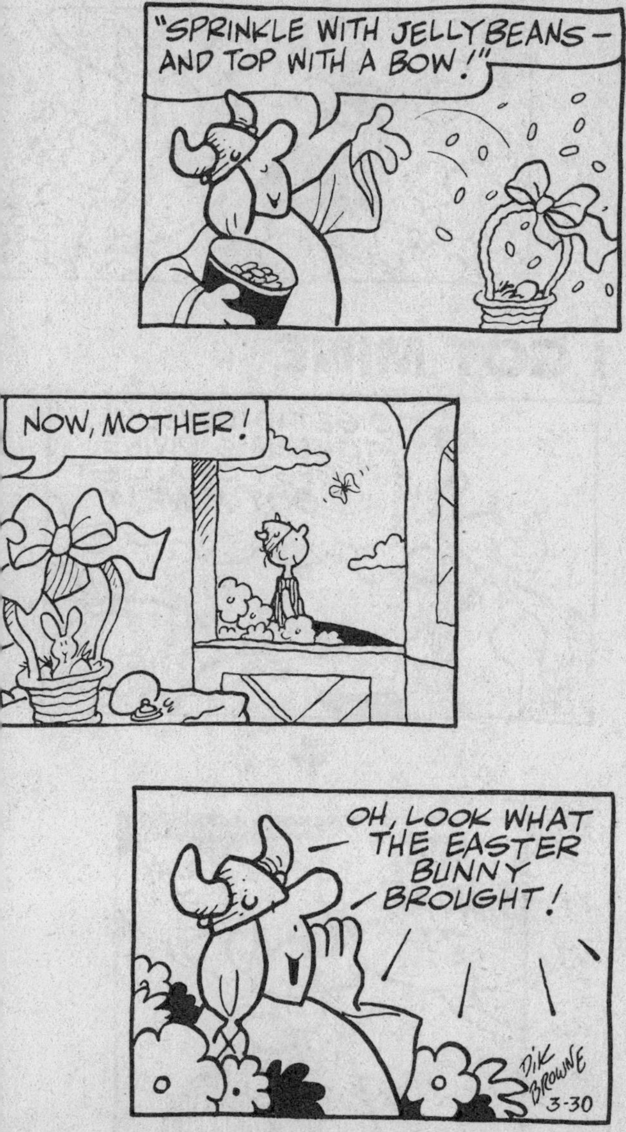
"SPRINKLE WITH JELLYBEANS — AND TOP WITH A BOW!"
NOW, MOTHER!
OH, LOOK WHAT THE EASTER BUNNY BROUGHT!
DIK BROWNE 3-30

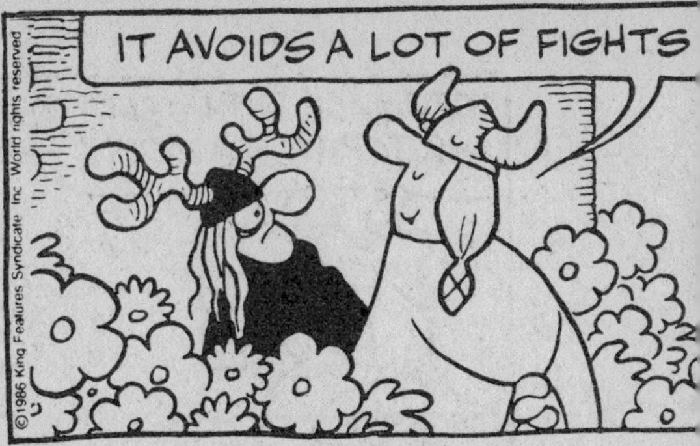
©1986 King Features Syndicate Inc World rights reserved
IT AVOIDS A LOT OF FIGHTS

I GOT MINE

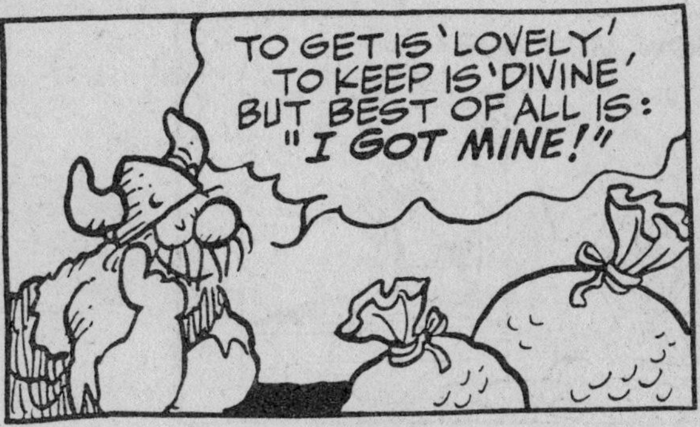
TO GET IS 'LOVELY', TO KEEP IS 'DIVINE' BUT BEST OF ALL IS: "I GOT MINE!"

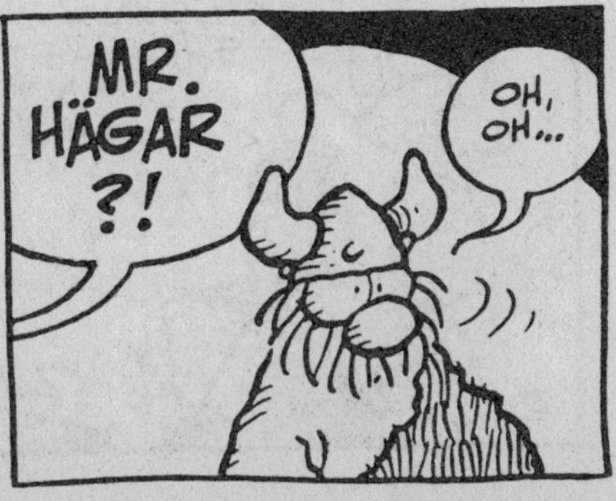
MR. HÄGAR ?!
OH, OH...

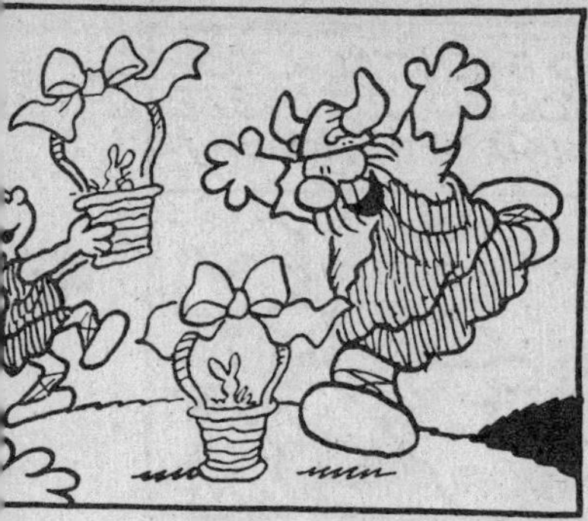

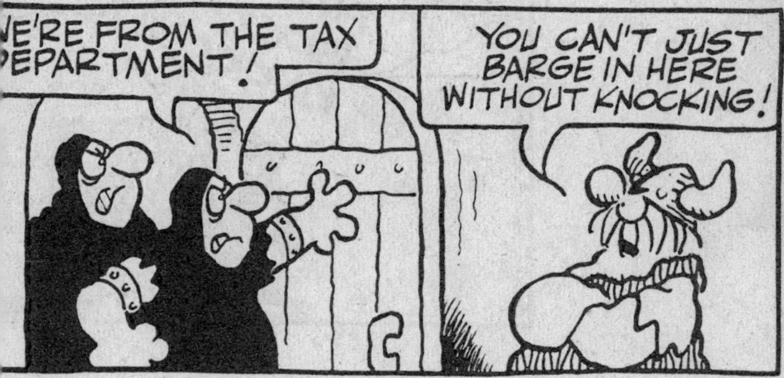
E'RE FROM THE TAX EPARTMENT!
YOU CAN'T JUST BARGE IN HERE WITHOUT KNOCKING!

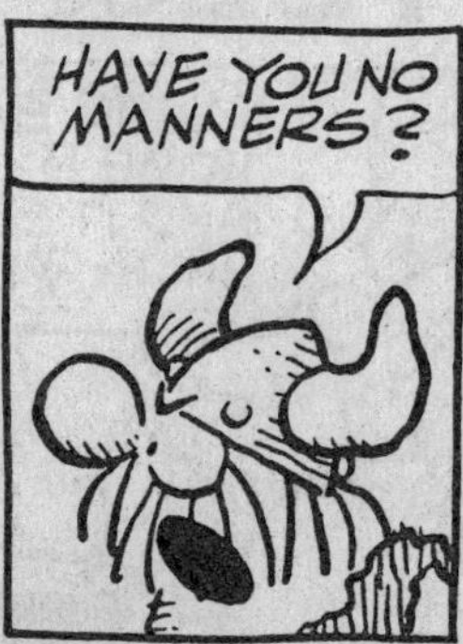
HAVE YOU NO MANNERS?

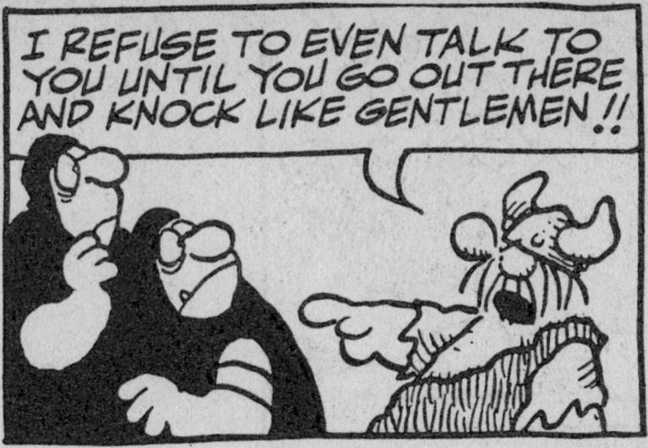
I REFUSE TO EVEN TALK TO YOU UNTIL YOU GO OUT THERE AND KNOCK LIKE GENTLEMEN !!

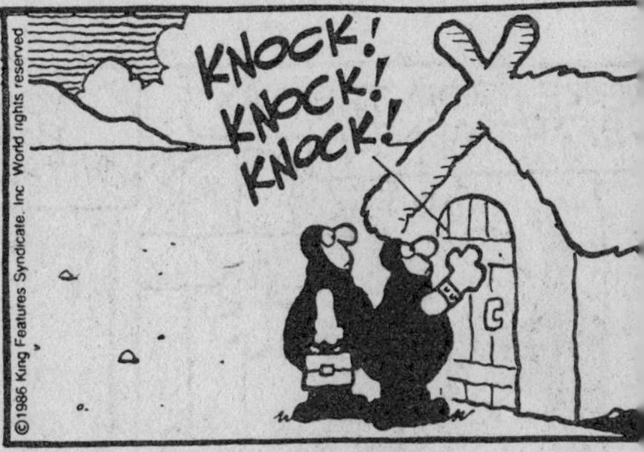
KNOCK! KNOCK! KNOCK!
©1986 King Features Syndicate, Inc. World rights reserved

RETURN POLICY

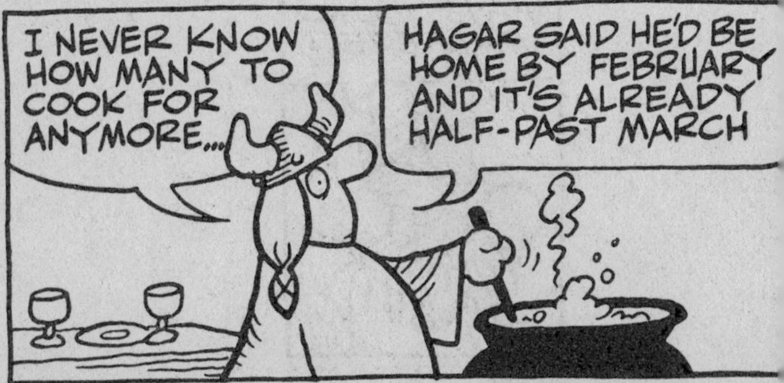
I NEVER KNOW HOW MANY TO COOK FOR ANYMORE...
HAGAR SAID HE'D BE HOME BY FEBRUARY AND IT'S ALREADY HALF-PAST MARCH

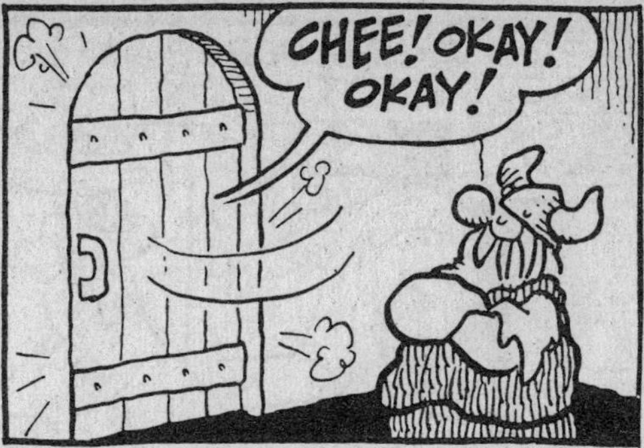
CHEE! OKAY! OKAY!

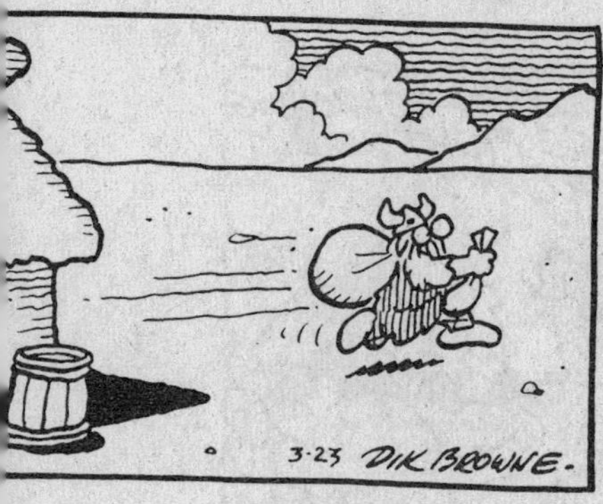
3-23 DIK BROWNE-

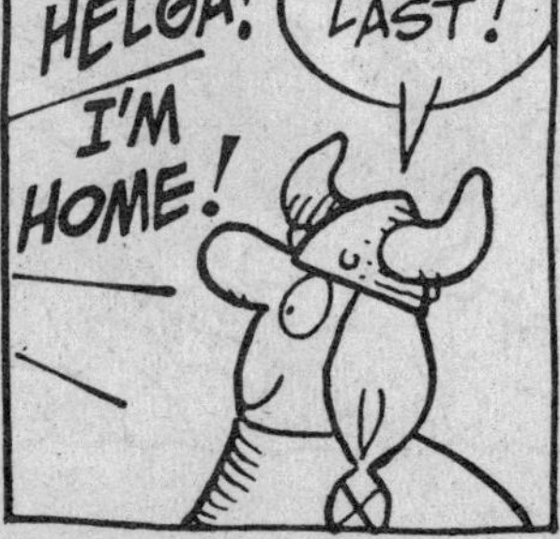
HELGA! I'M HOME!
AT LAST!

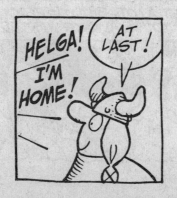

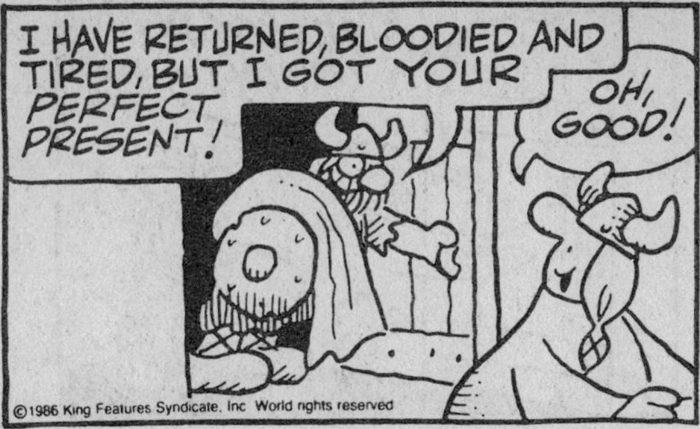
I HAVE RETURNED, BLOODIED AND TIRED, BUT I GOT YOUR PERFECT PRESENT!
OH, GOOD!

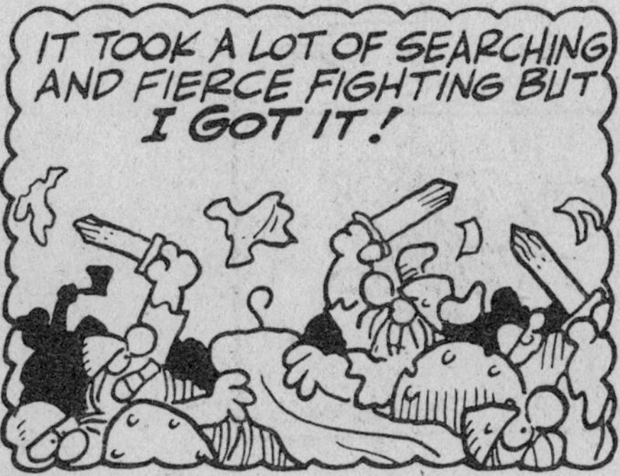
IT TOOK A LOT OF SEARCHING AND FIERCE FIGHTING BUT I GOT IT!

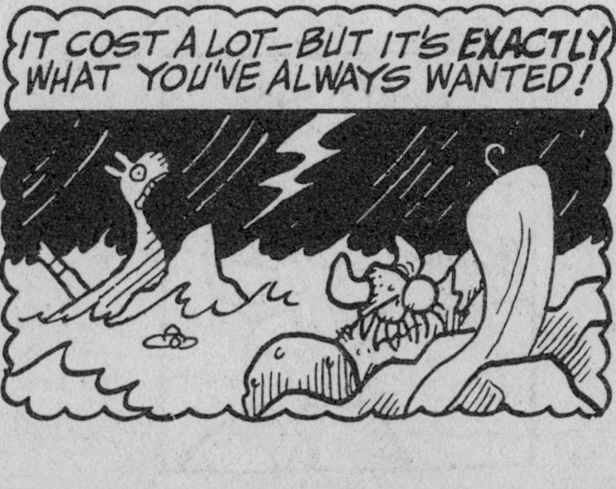
IT COST A LOT—BUT IT'S EXACTLY WHAT YOU'VE ALWAYS WANTED!

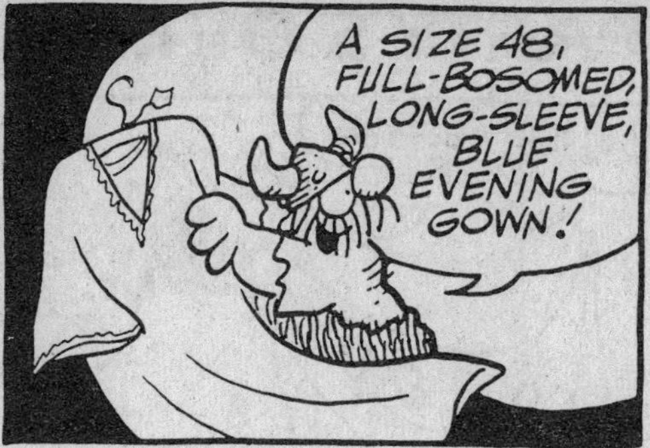
A SIZE 48, FULL-BOSOMED, LONG-SLEEVE, BLUE EVENING GOWN!

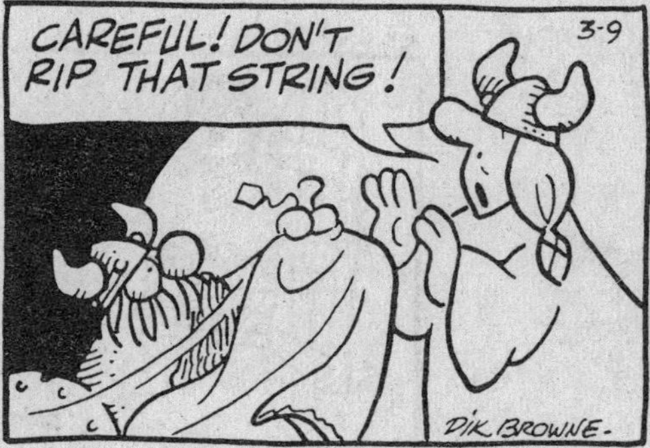
CAREFUL! DON'T RIP THAT STRING!
3-9
DIK BROWNE

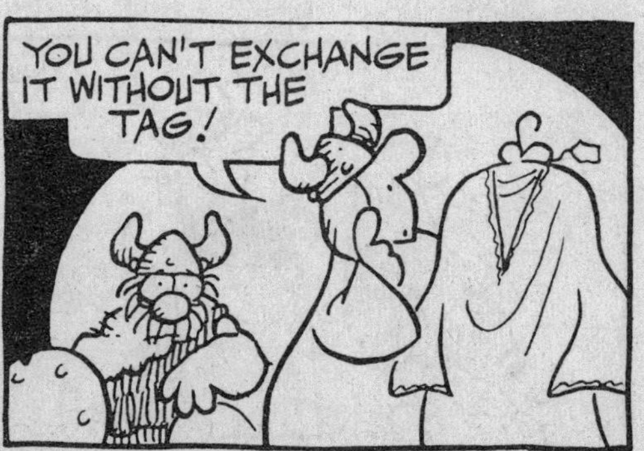
YOU CAN'T EXCHANGE IT WITHOUT THE TAG!

PARTY'S OVER

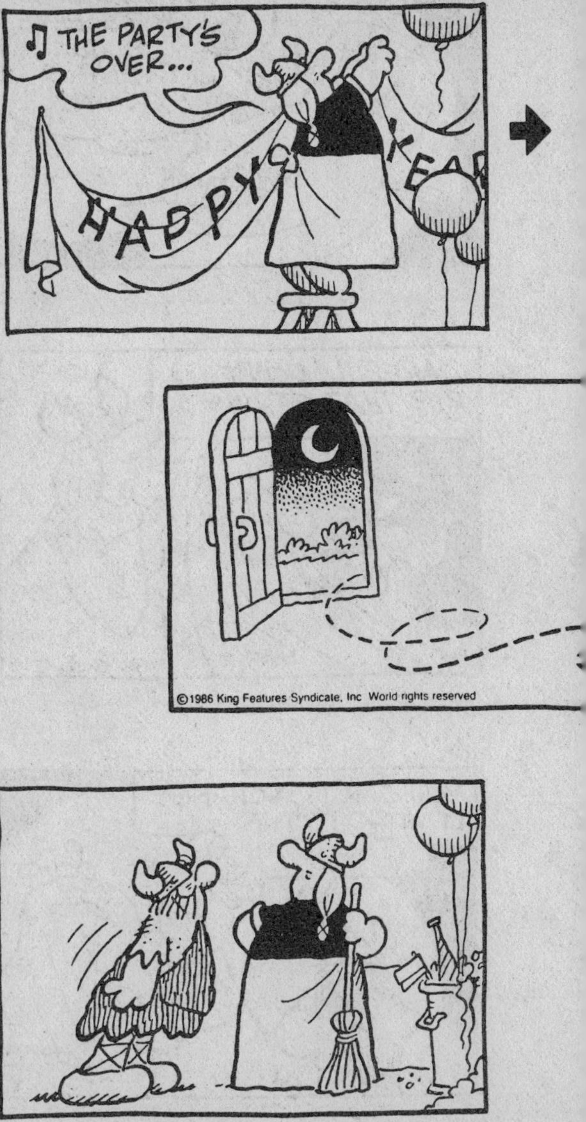
♫ THE PARTY'S OVER...
HAPPY YEAR
©1986 King Features Syndicate, Inc World rights reserved

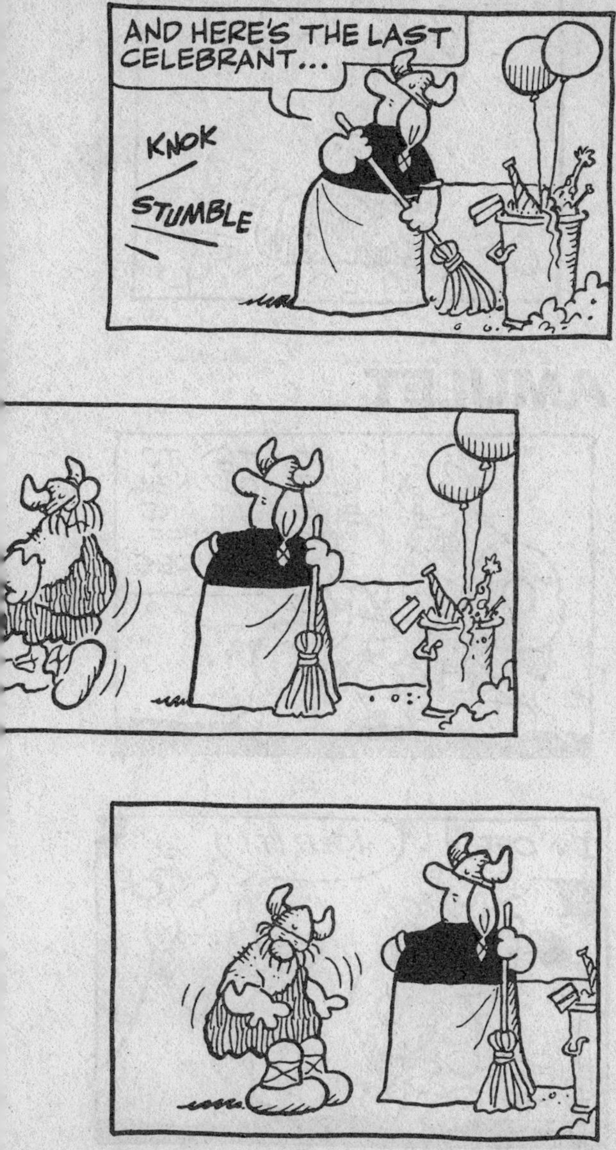
AND HERE'S THE LAST CELEBRANT...
KNOK
STUMBLE

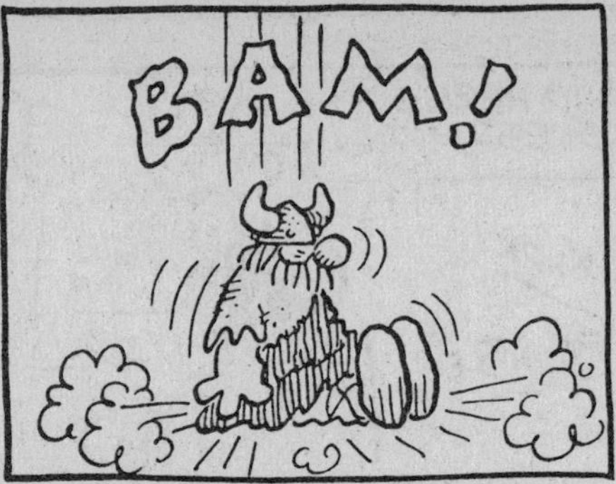
BAM!

AMULET

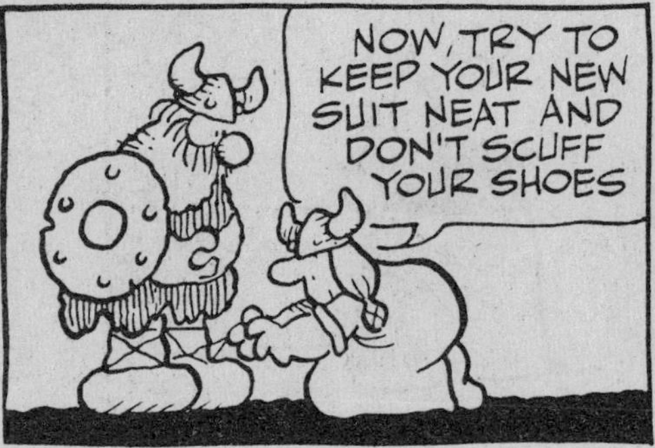
NOW, TRY TO KEEP YOUR NEW SUIT NEAT AND DON'T SCUFF YOUR SHOES

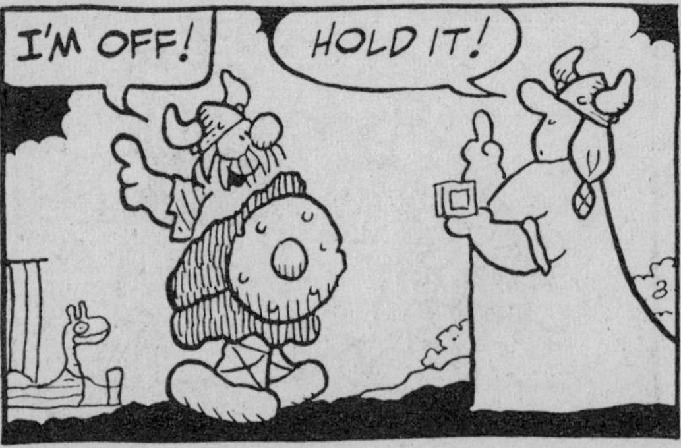
I'M OFF!
HOLD IT!

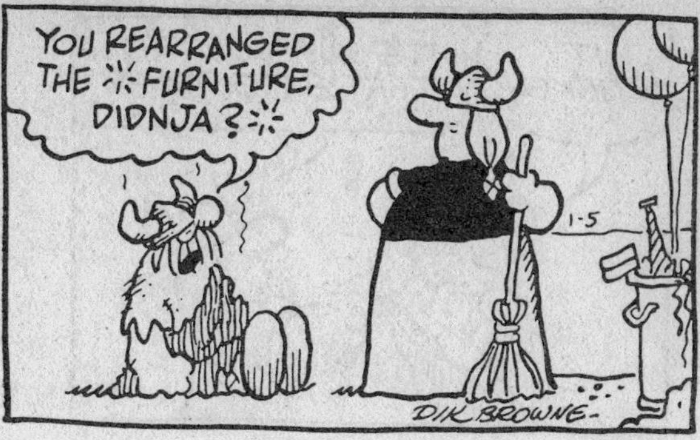
YOU REARRANGED THE FURNITURE, DIDNJA?
1-5
DIK BROWNE

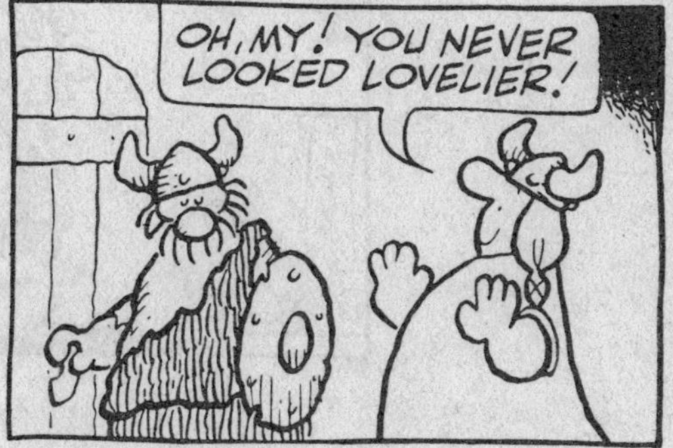
OH, MY! YOU NEVER LOOKED LOVELIER!

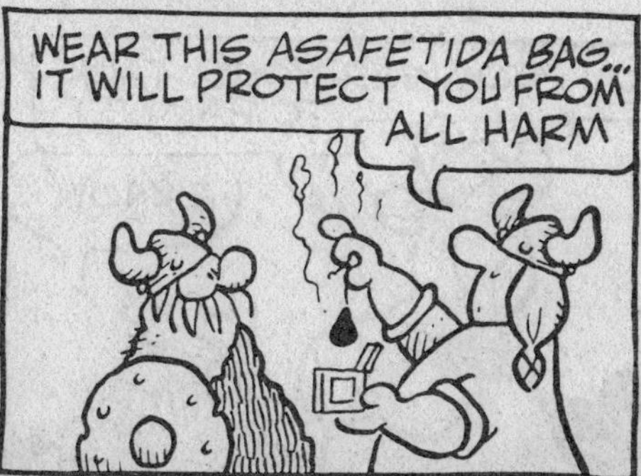
WEAR THIS ASAFETIDA BAG... IT WILL PROTECT YOU FROM ALL HARM

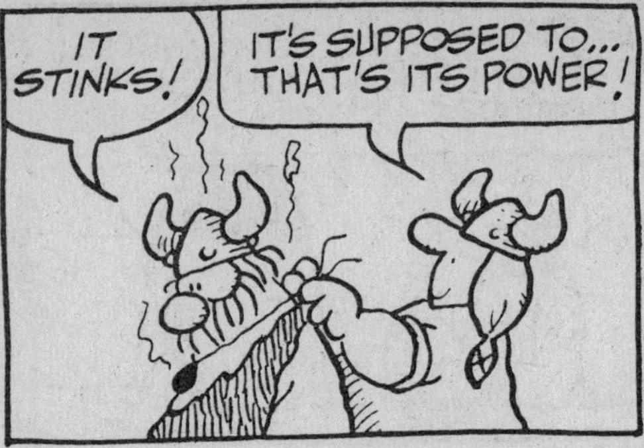
IT STINKS!
IT'S SUPPOSED TO... THAT'S ITS POWER!

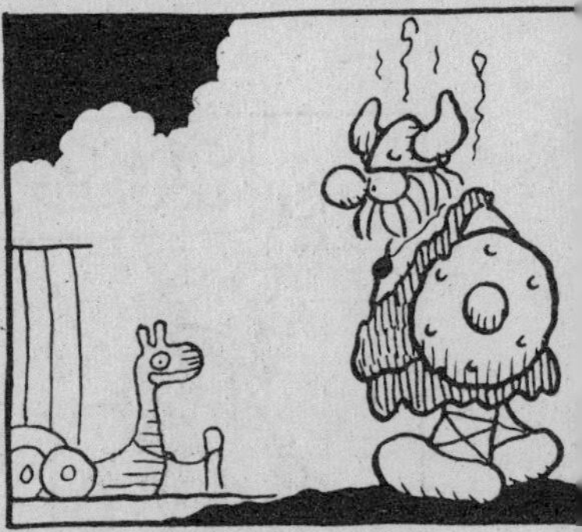

FACTS OF LIFE

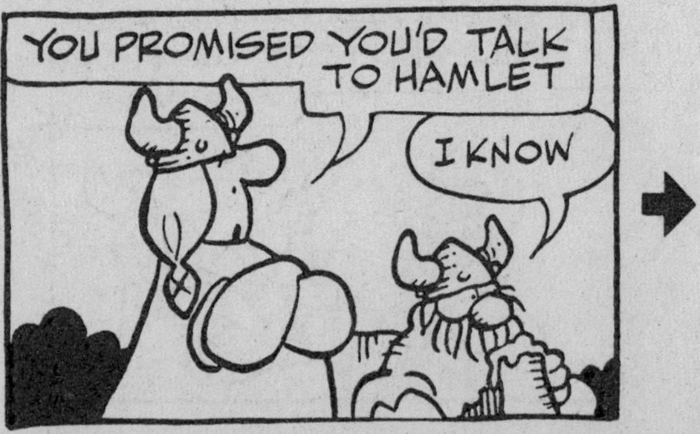
YOU PROMISED YOU'D TALK TO HAMLET
I KNOW

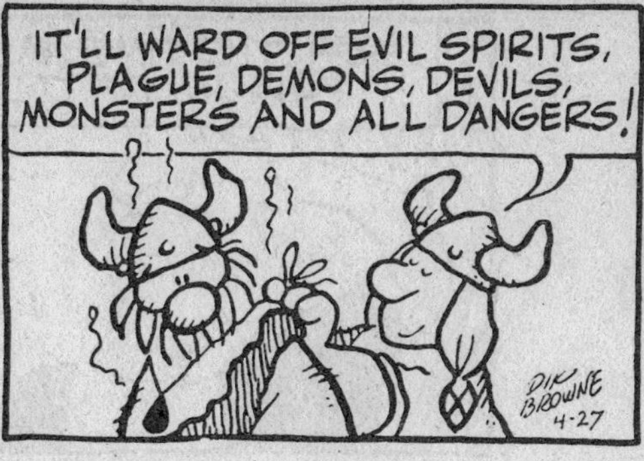
IT'LL WARD OFF EVIL SPIRITS, PLAGUE, DEMONS, DEVILS, MONSTERS AND ALL DANGERS!
DIK BROWNE 4-27

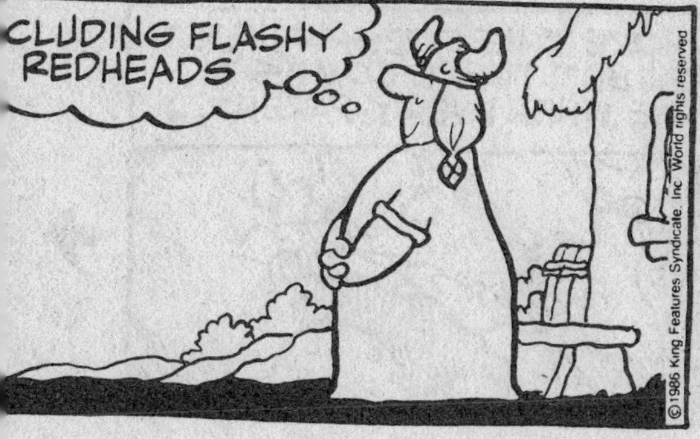
CLUDING FLASHY REDHEADS
© 1986 King Features Syndicate, Inc. World rights reserved

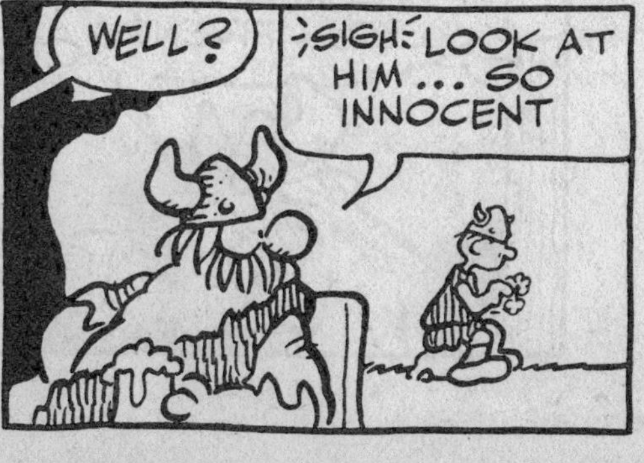
WELL?
-SIGH- LOOK AT HIM ... SO INNOCENT

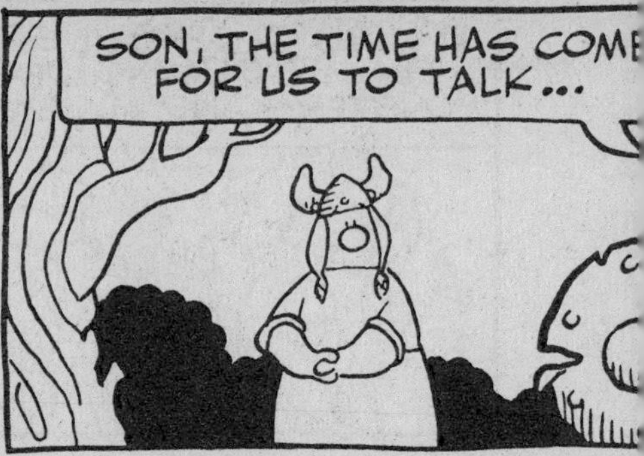
SON, THE TIME HAS COM
FOR US TO TALK...

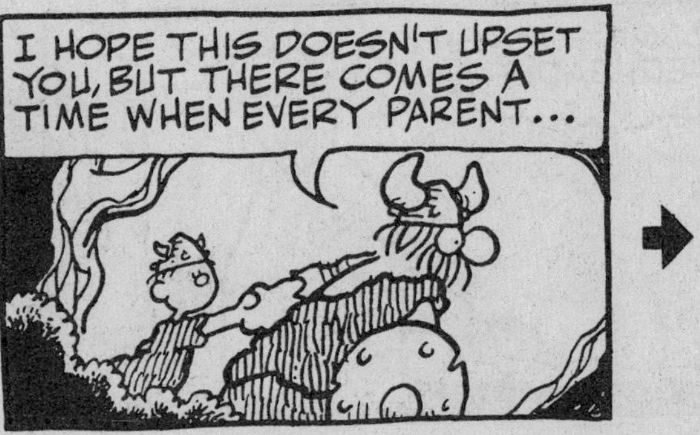
I HOPE THIS DOESN'T UPSET YOU, BUT THERE COMES A TIME WHEN EVERY PARENT...

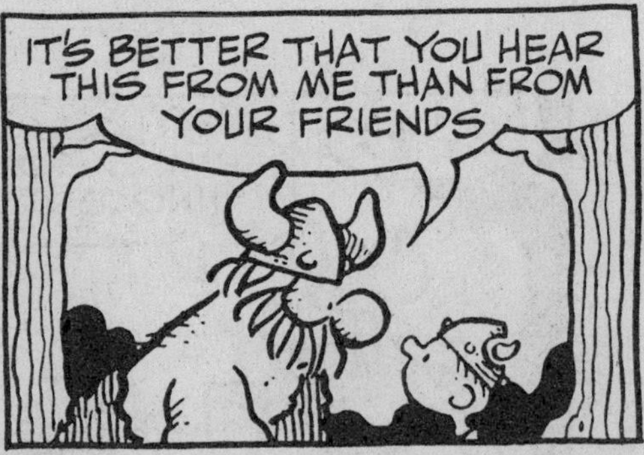
IT'S BETTER THAT YOU HEAR THIS FROM ME THAN FROM YOUR FRIENDS

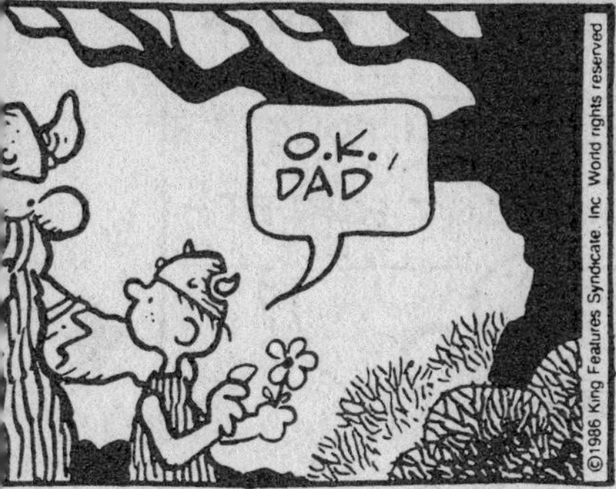
O.K., DAD
©1986 King Features Syndicate, Inc. World rights reserved

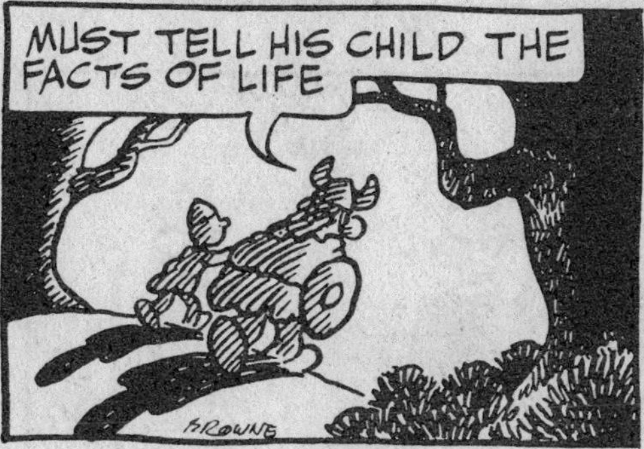
MUST TELL HIS CHILD THE FACTS OF LIFE
BROWNE

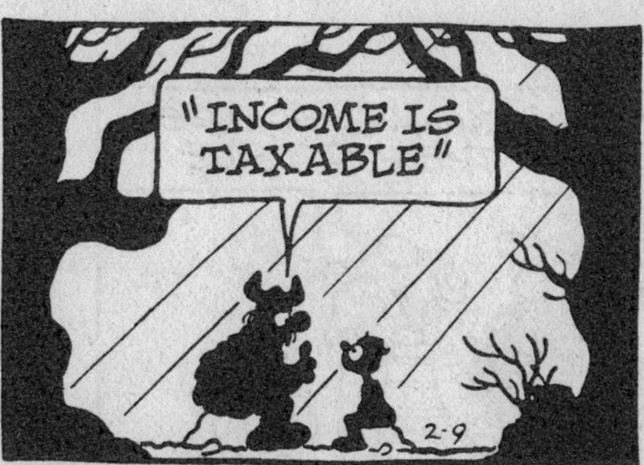
"INCOME IS TAXABLE"
2-9

NAME DROPPING

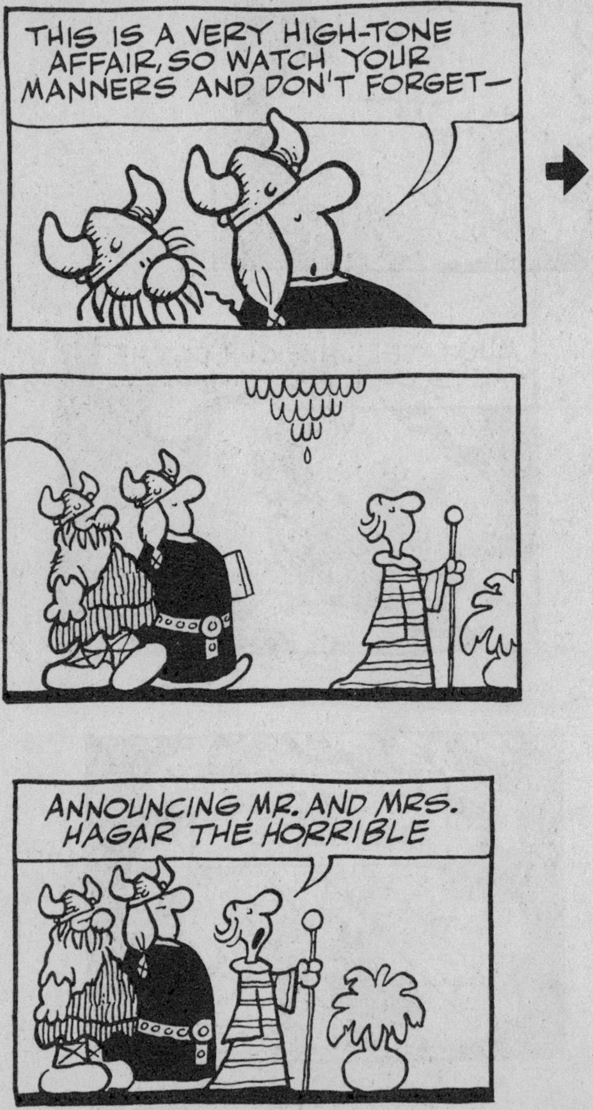
THIS IS A VERY HIGH-TONE AFFAIR, SO WATCH YOUR MANNERS AND DON'T FORGET—
ANNOUNCING MR. AND MRS. HAGAR THE HORRIBLE

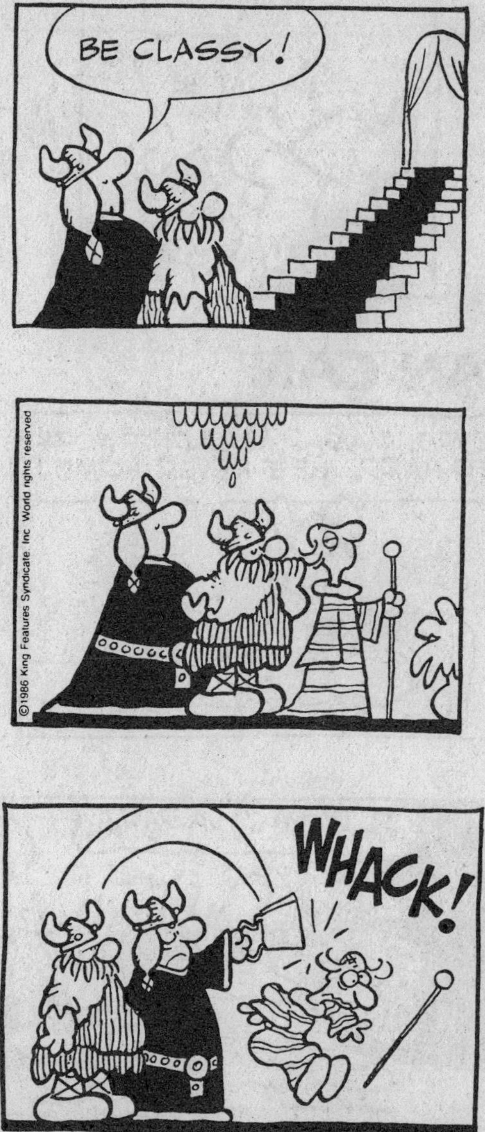
BE CLASSY!
©1986 King Features Syndicate, Inc. World rights reserved
WHACK!

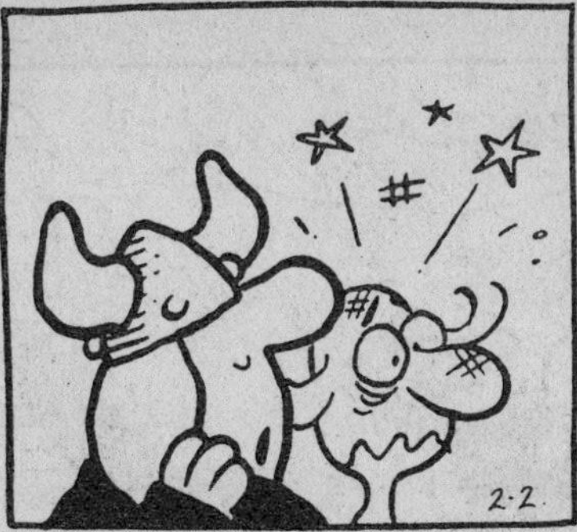
2·2.

CAN-CAN

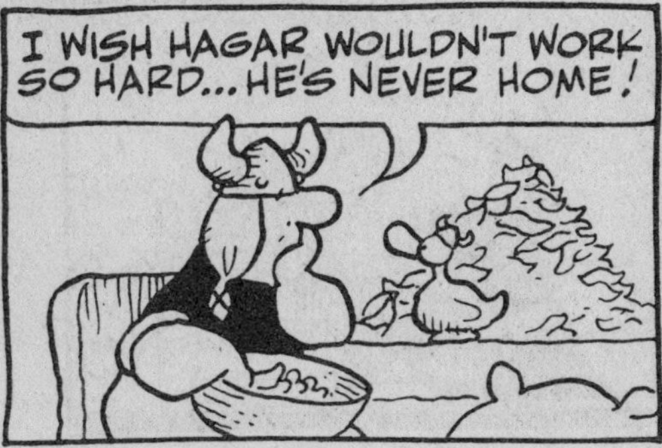
I WISH HAGAR WOULDN'T WORK SO HARD... HE'S NEVER HOME!

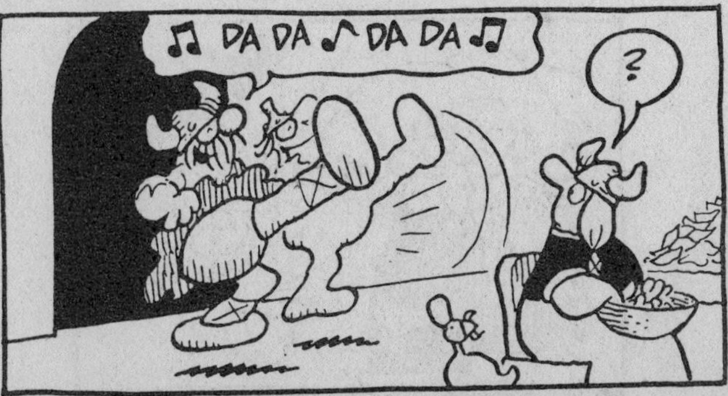
♫ DA DA ♪ DA DA ♫
?

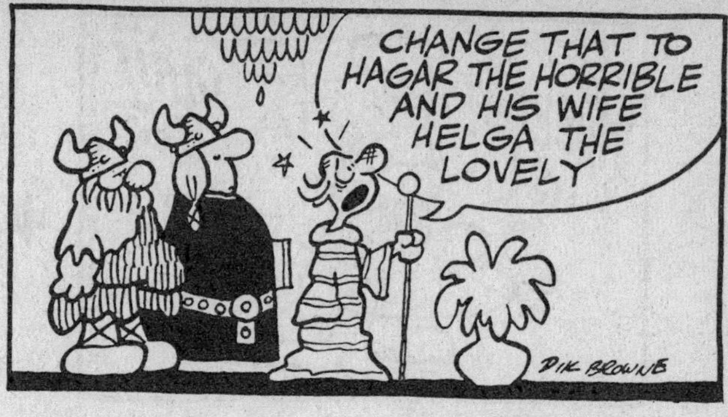
CHANGE THAT TO HAGAR THE HORRIBLE AND HIS WIFE HELGA THE LOVELY
DIK BROWNE

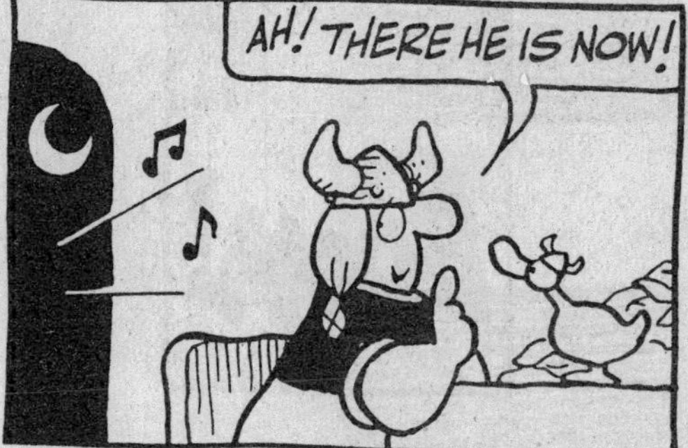
AH! THERE HE IS NOW!

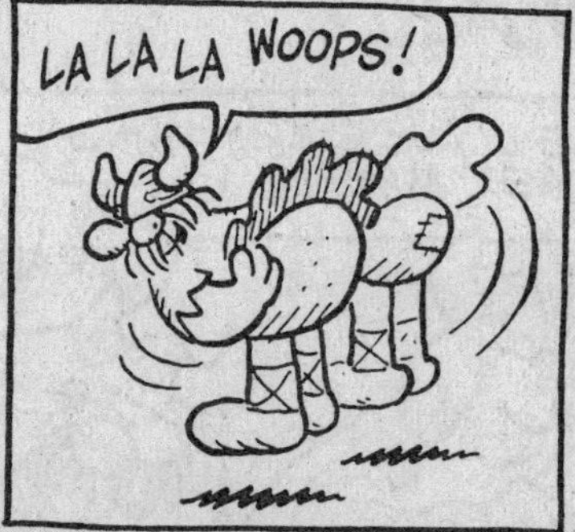
LA LA LA WOOPS!

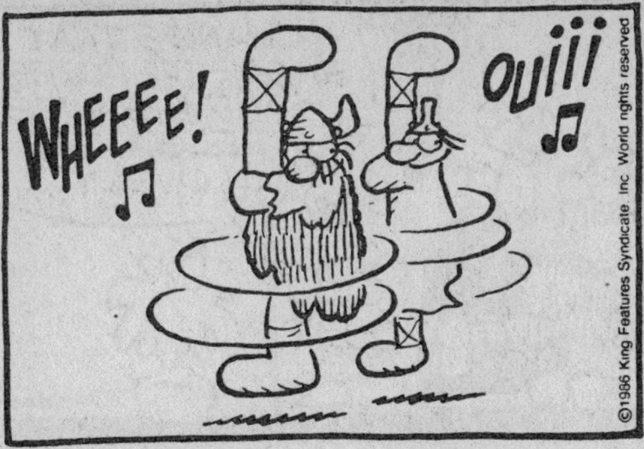
WHEEEEE!
OUIIII
©1986 King Features Syndicate, Inc. World rights reserved

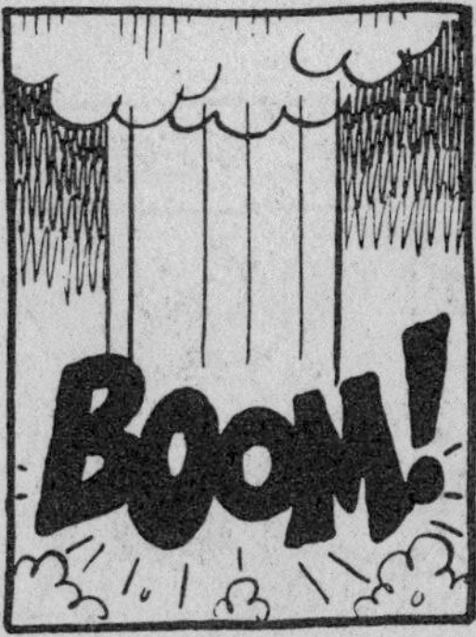
BOOM!

AIR MAIL

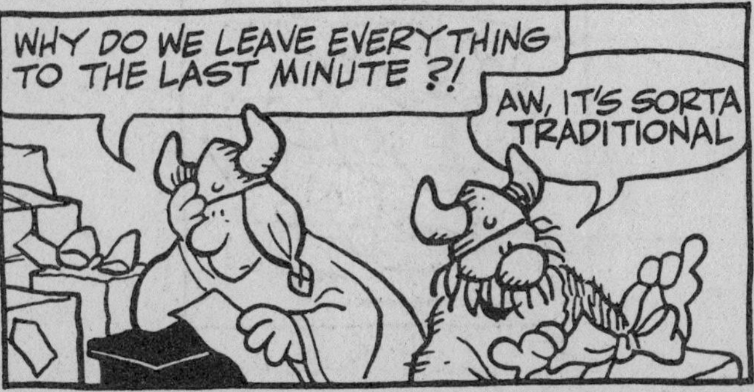
WHY DO WE LEAVE EVERYTHING TO THE LAST MINUTE ?!
AW, IT'S SORTA TRADITIONAL

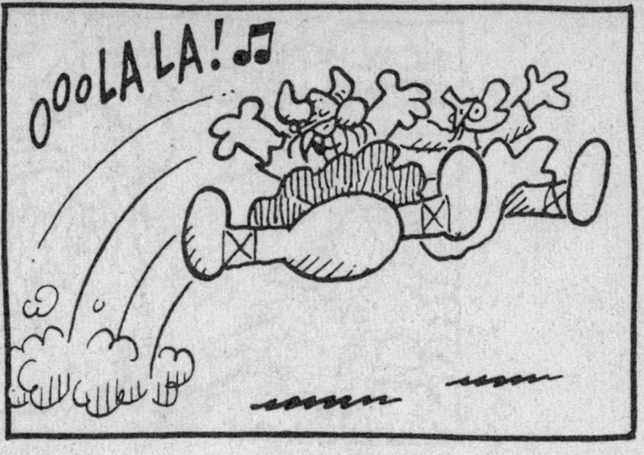
OOOLA LA! ♫

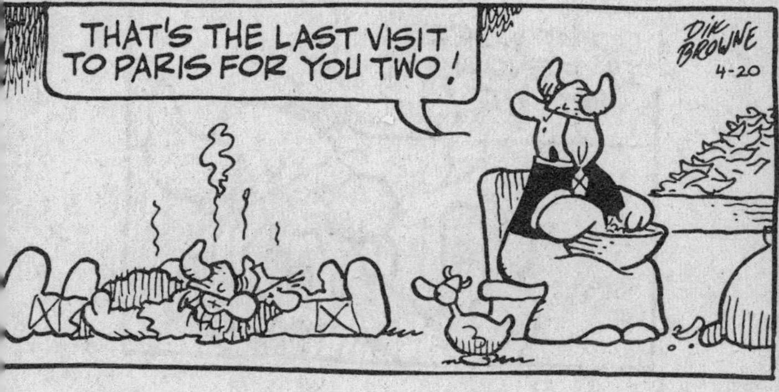
THAT'S THE LAST VISIT TO PARIS FOR YOU TWO!
DIK BROWNE
4-20

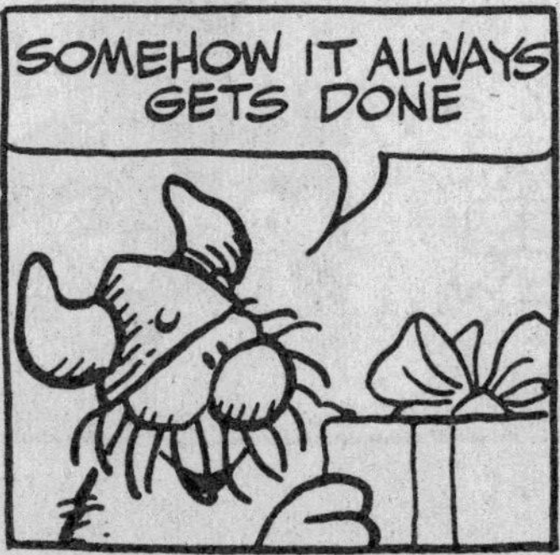
SOMEHOW IT ALWAYS GETS DONE

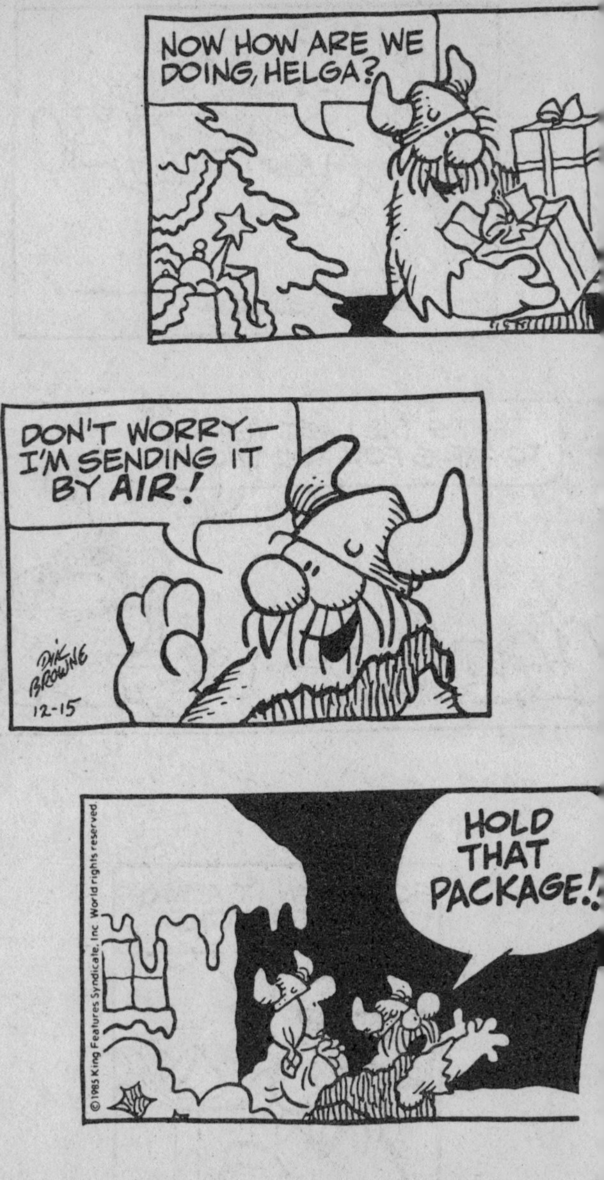
NOW HOW ARE WE DOING, HELGA?
DON'T WORRY— I'M SENDING IT BY AIR!
DIK BROWNE
12-15
HOLD THAT PACKAGE!
©1985 King Features Syndicate, Inc. World rights reserved.

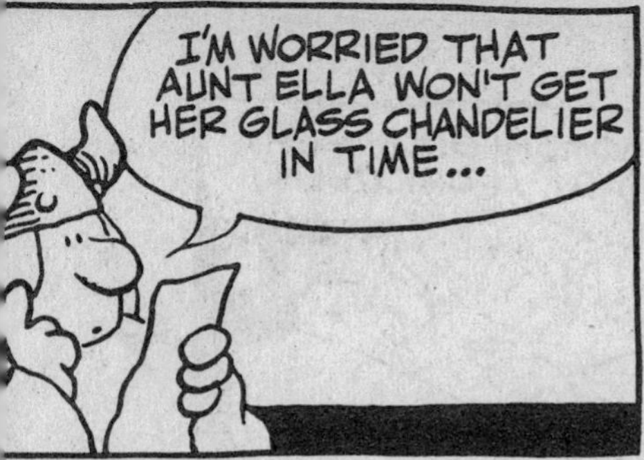
I'M WORRIED THAT AUNT ELLA WON'T GET HER GLASS CHANDELIER IN TIME...

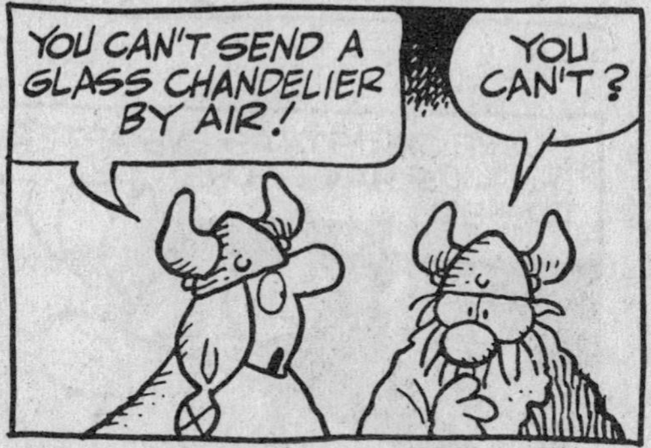
YOU CAN'T SEND A GLASS CHANDELIER BY AIR!
YOU CAN'T ?

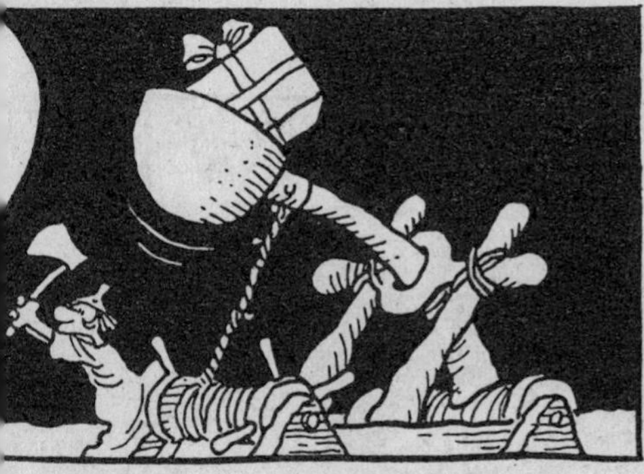

NOËL

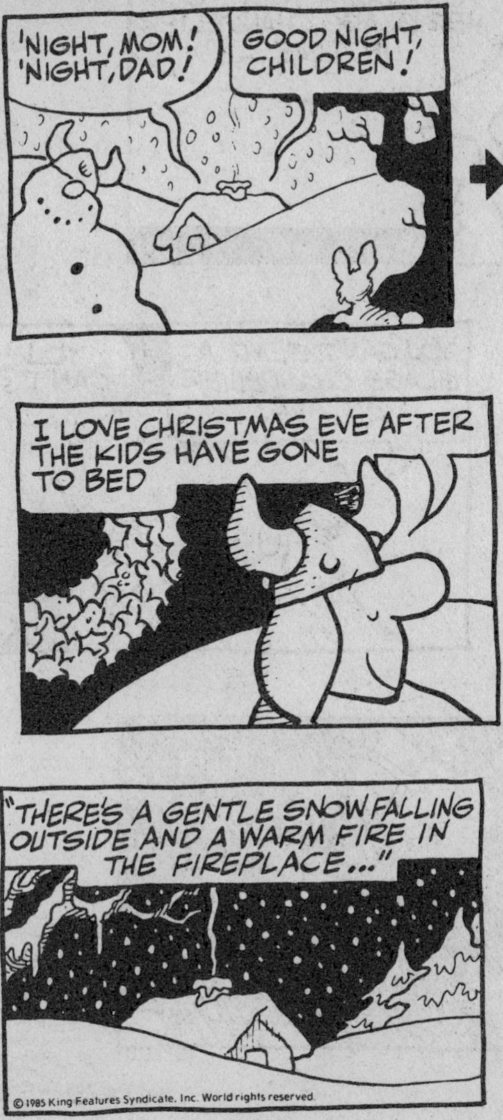

'NIGHT, MOM! 'NIGHT, DAD!
GOOD NIGHT, CHILDREN!
I LOVE CHRISTMAS EVE AFTER THE KIDS HAVE GONE TO BED
"THERE'S A GENTLE SNOW FALLING OUTSIDE AND A WARM FIRE IN THE FIREPLACE..."

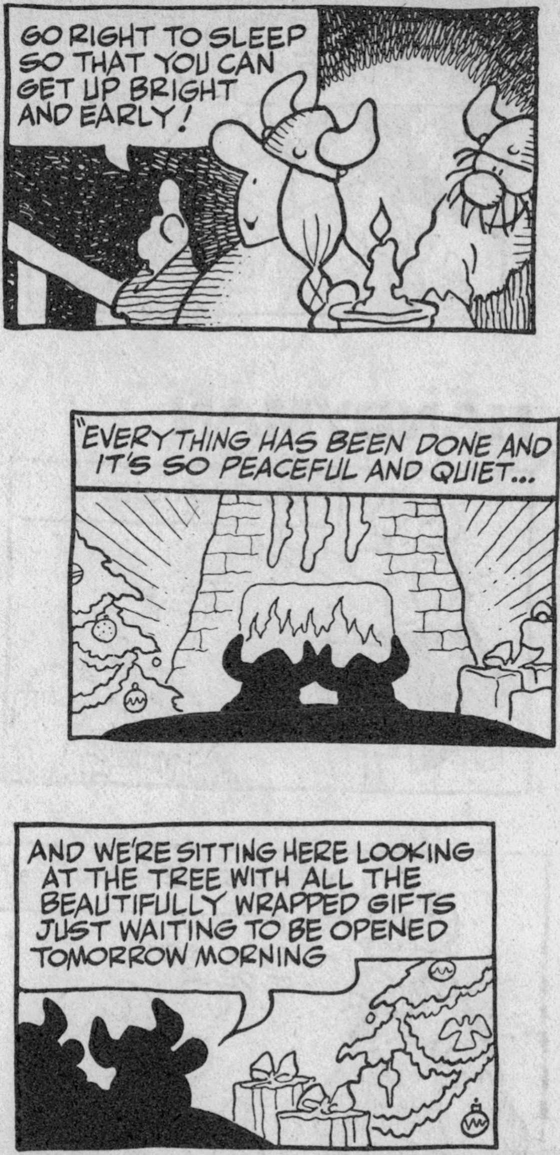
GO RIGHT TO SLEEP SO THAT YOU CAN GET UP BRIGHT AND EARLY!
"EVERYTHING HAS BEEN DONE AND IT'S SO PEACEFUL AND QUIET...
AND WE'RE SITTING HERE LOOKING AT THE TREE WITH ALL THE BEAUTIFULLY WRAPPED GIFTS JUST WAITING TO BE OPENED TOMORROW MORNING

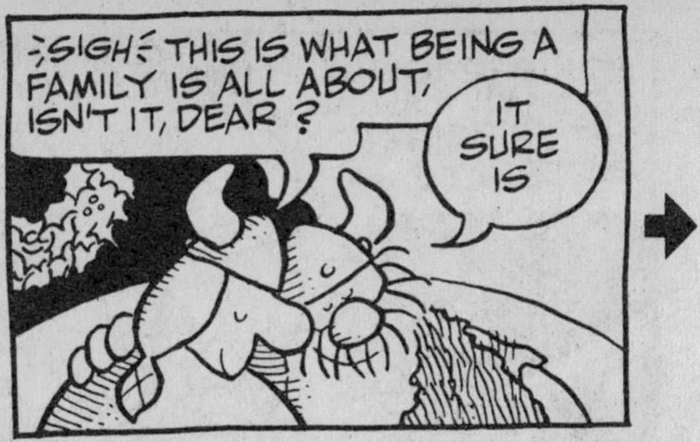
-;SIGH-; THIS IS WHAT BEING A FAMILY IS ALL ABOUT, ISN'T IT, DEAR ?
IT SURE IS

HANDYMAN

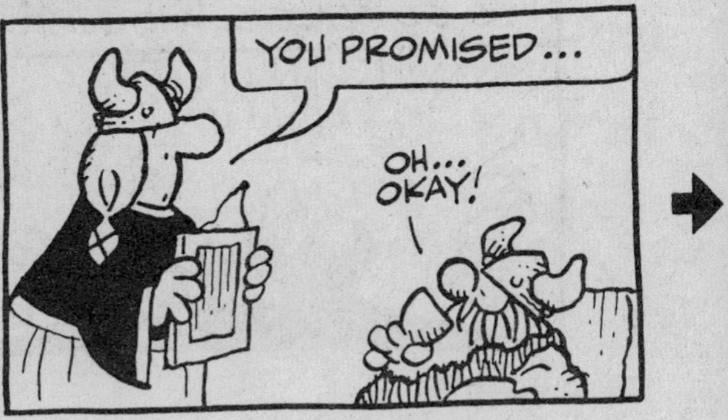
YOU PROMISED...
OH... OKAY!

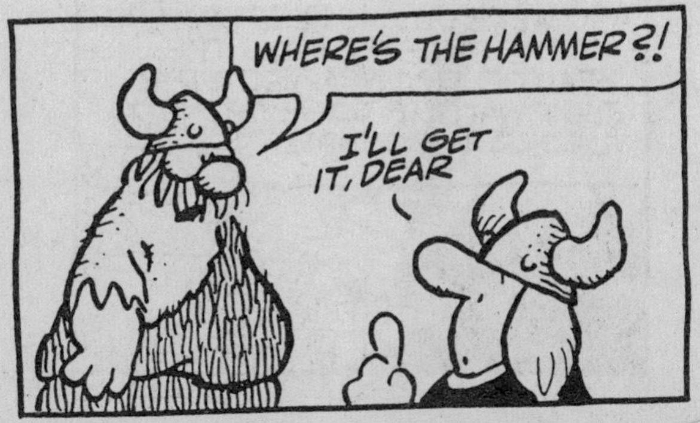
WHERE'S THE HAMMER ?!
I'LL GET IT, DEAR

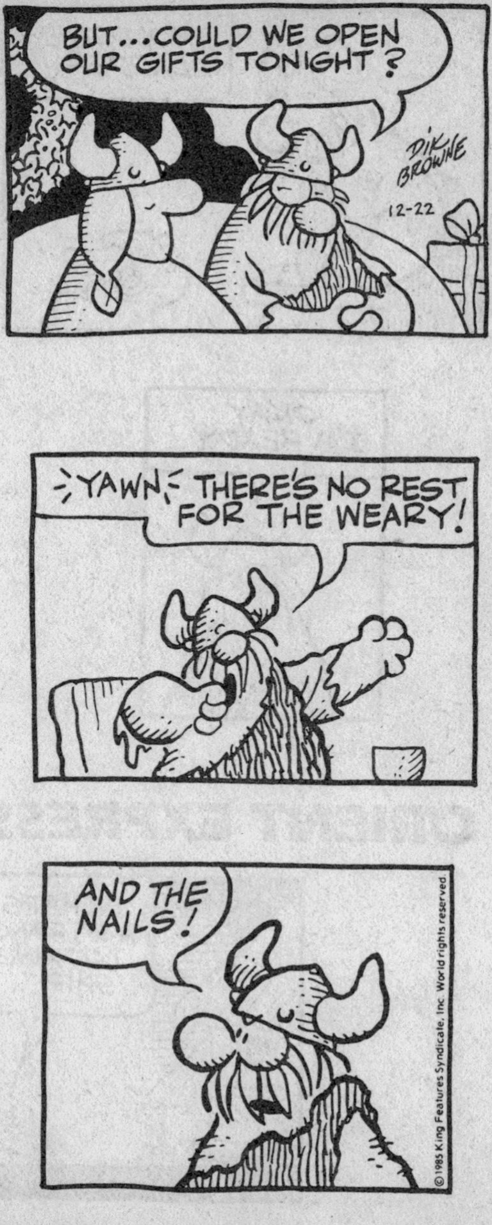
BUT...COULD WE OPEN OUR GIFTS TONIGHT?
DIK BROWNE
12-22
YAWN THERE'S NO REST FOR THE WEARY!
AND THE NAILS!
© 1985 King Features Syndicate, Inc. World rights reserved.

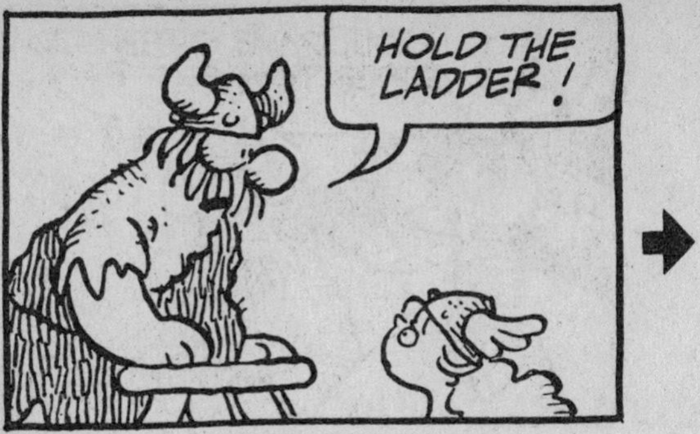
HOLD THE LADDER!

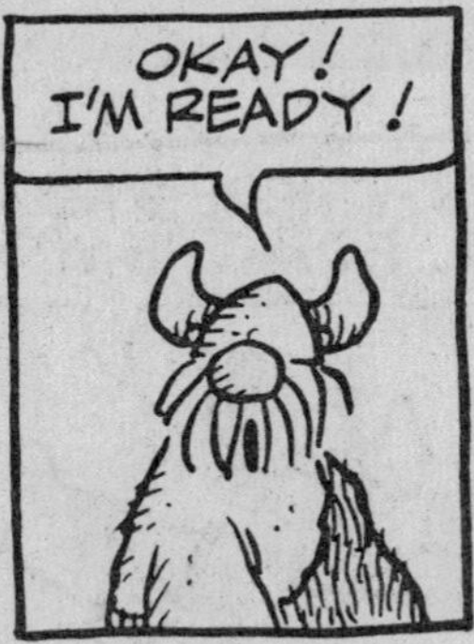
OKAY! I'M READY!

ORIENT EXPRESS

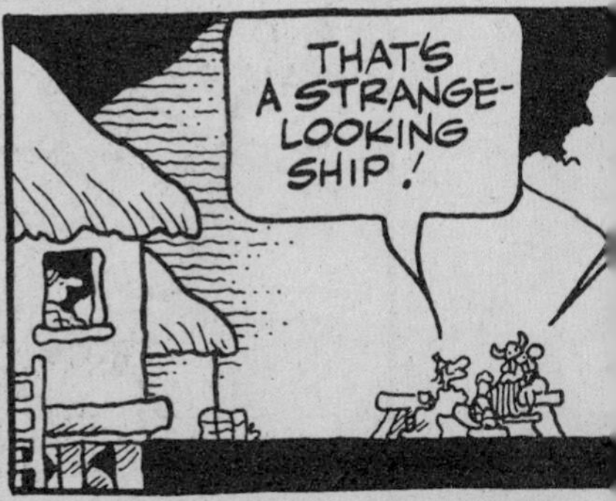
THAT'S A STRANGE-LOOKING SHIP!

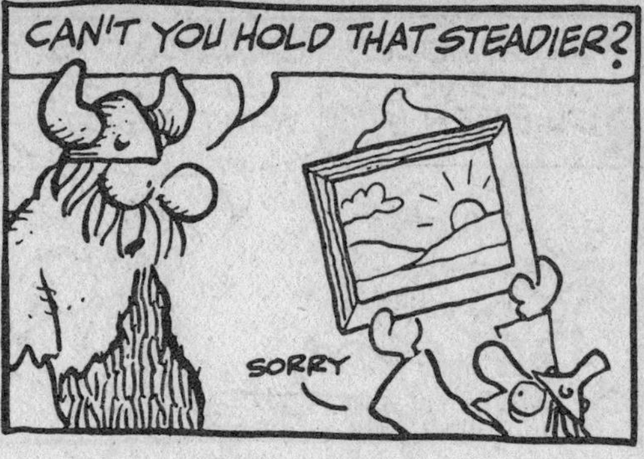
CAN'T YOU HOLD THAT STEADIER?
SORRY

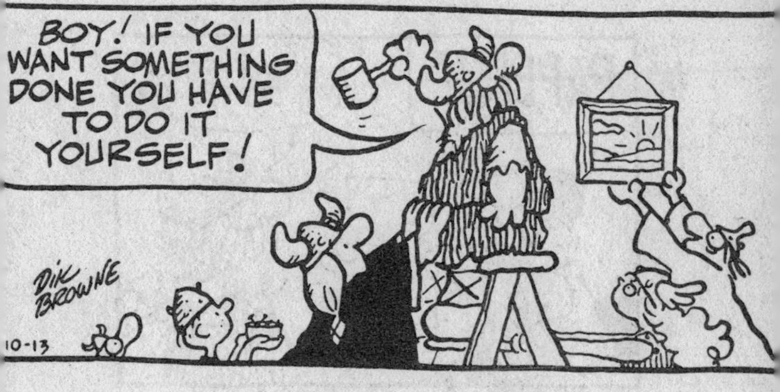
BOY! IF YOU WANT SOMETHING DONE YOU HAVE TO DO IT YOURSELF!
DIK BROWNE
10-13

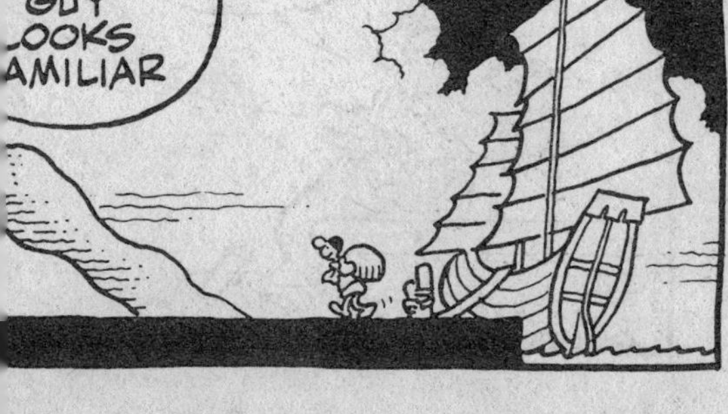
UT THAT GUY LOOKS AMILIAR

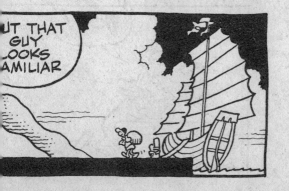

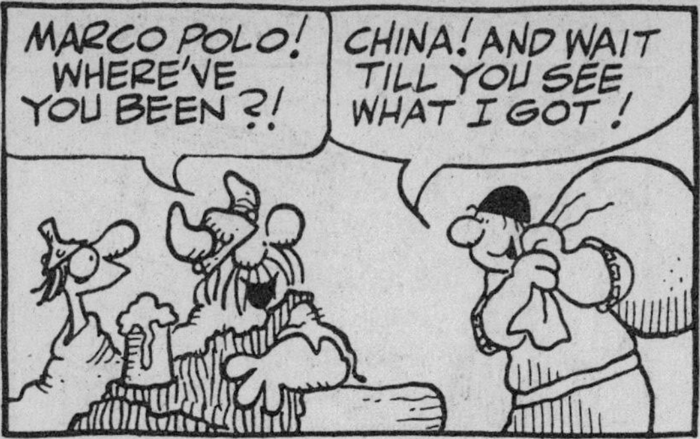
MARCO POLO! WHERE'VE YOU BEEN ?!
CHINA! AND WAIT TILL YOU SEE WHAT I GOT !

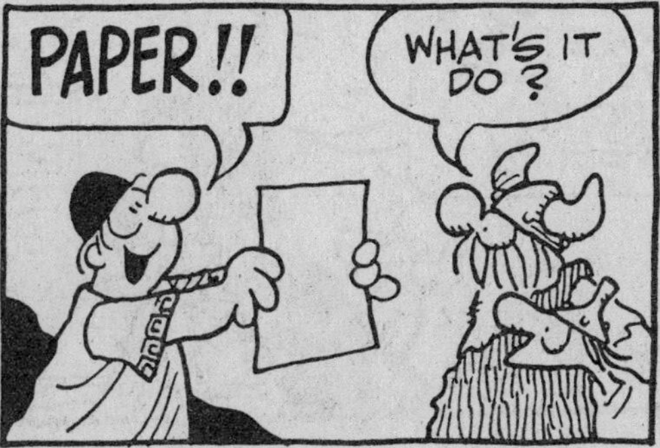
PAPER!!
WHAT'S IT DO ?

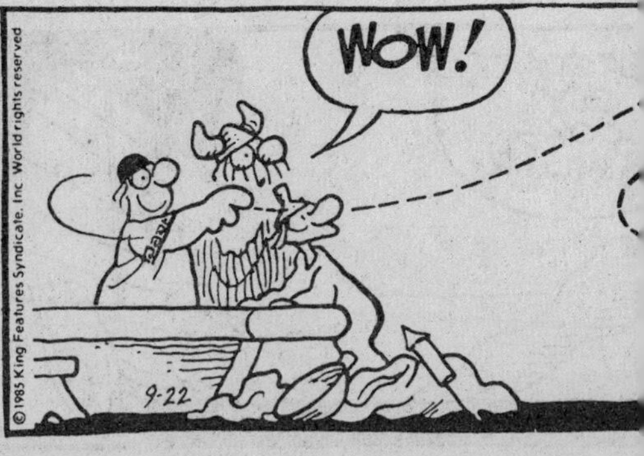
WOW!
9-22
© 1985 King Features Syndicate, Inc. World rights reserved

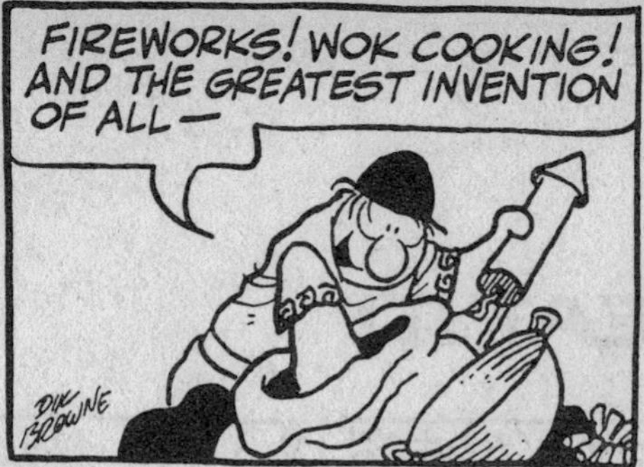
FIREWORKS! WOK COOKING! AND THE GREATEST INVENTION OF ALL—
DIK BROWNE

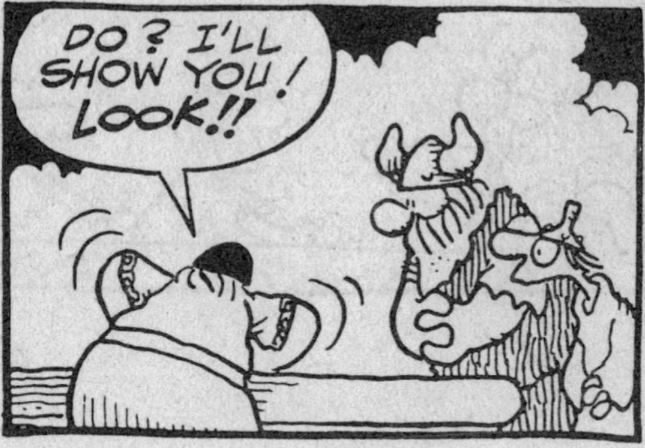
DO? I'LL SHOW YOU! LOOK!!

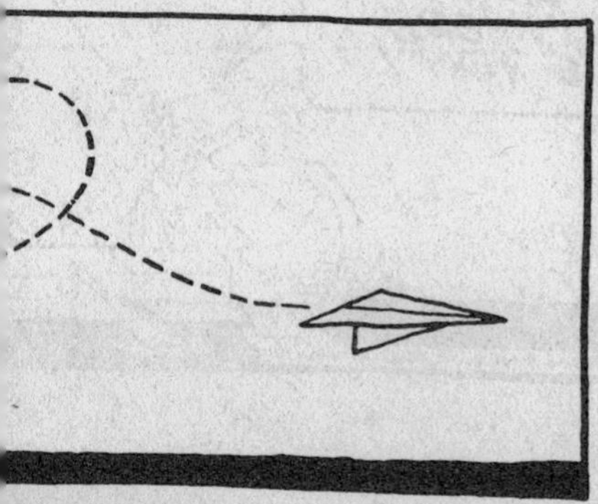

BEAT IT!

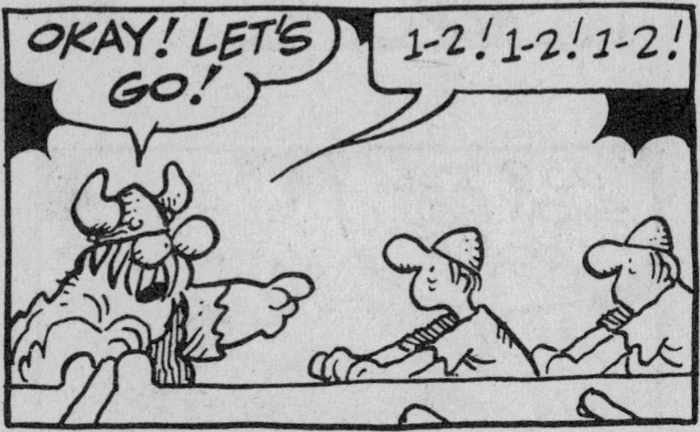
OKAY! LET'S GO!
1-2! 1-2! 1-2!

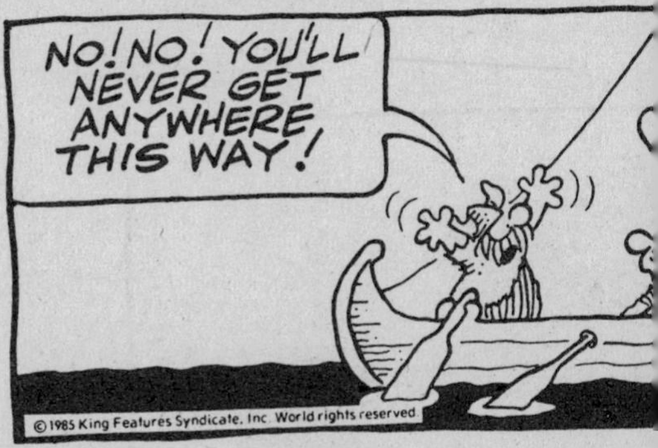
NO! NO! YOU'LL NEVER GET ANYWHERE THIS WAY!
© 1985 King Features Syndicate, Inc. World rights reserved

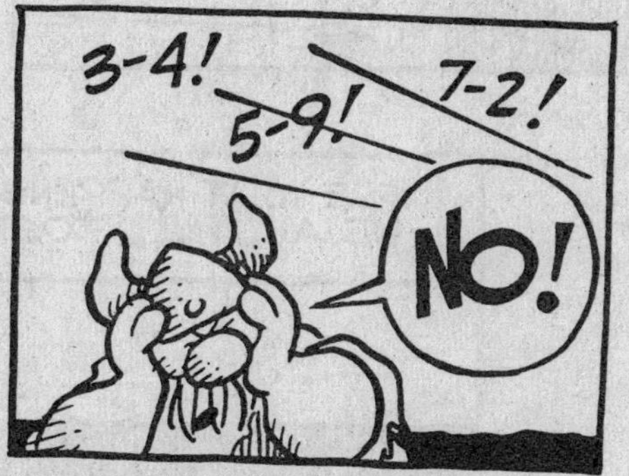
3-4!
5-9!
7-2!
NO!

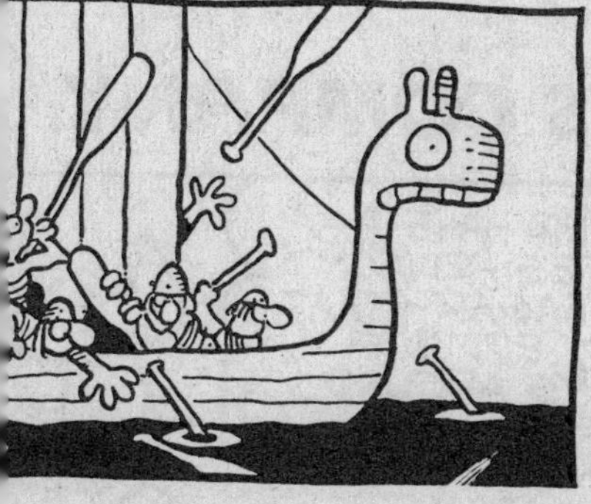

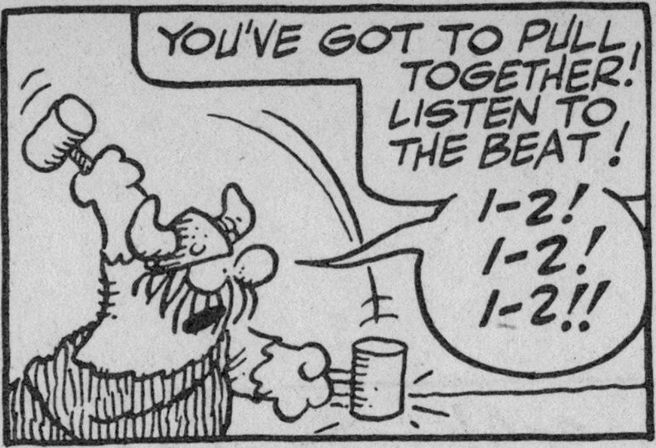
YOU'VE GOT TO PULL TOGETHER! LISTEN TO THE BEAT!
1-2! 1-2! 1-2!!

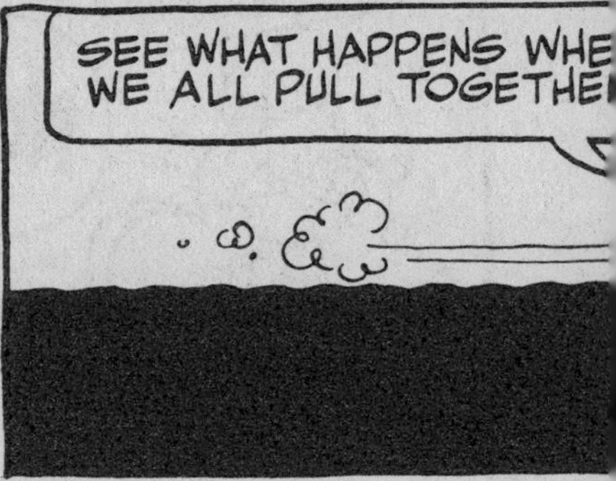
SEE WHAT HAPPENS WHE
WE ALL PULL TOGETHE

TWO'S COMPANY

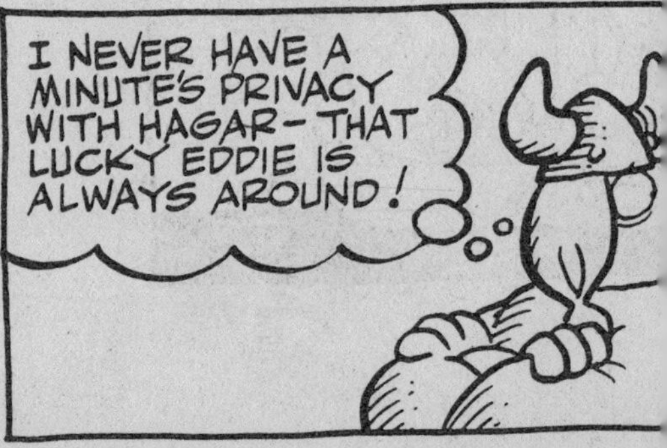
I NEVER HAVE A MINUTE'S PRIVACY WITH HAGAR– THAT LUCKY EDDIE IS ALWAYS AROUND!

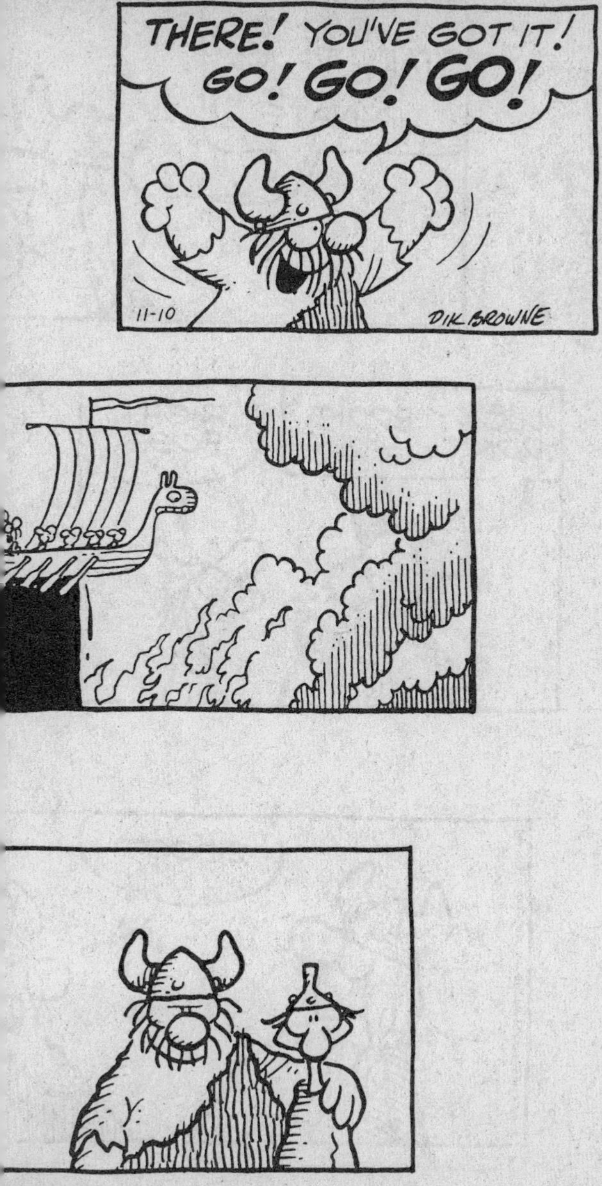

THERE! YOU'VE GOT IT! GO! GO! GO!
11-10
DIK BROWNE

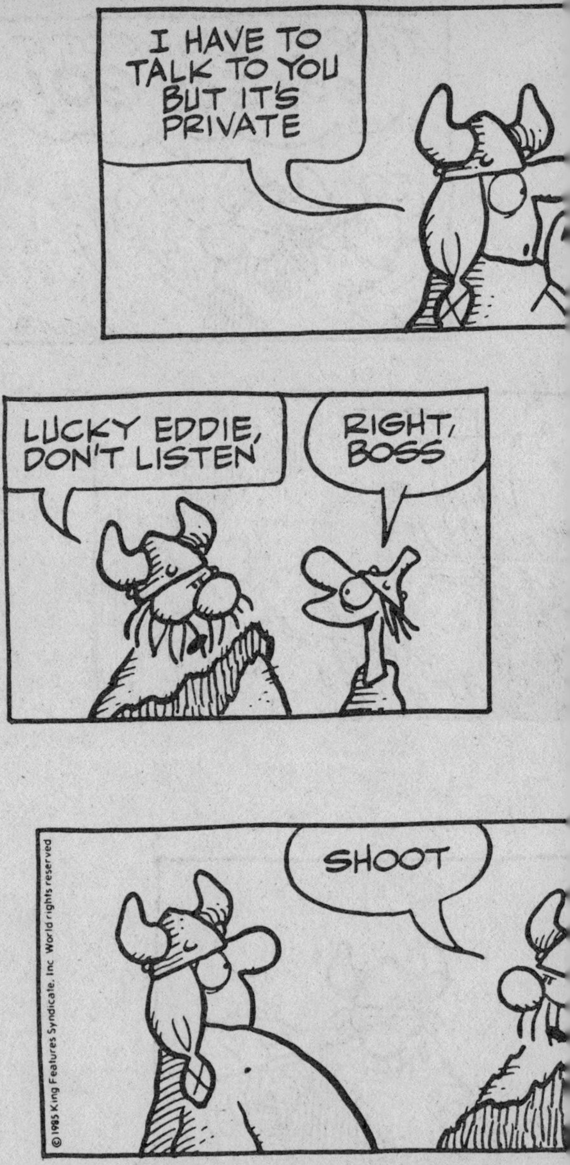
I HAVE TO TALK TO YOU BUT IT'S PRIVATE
LUCKY EDDIE, DON'T LISTEN
RIGHT, BOSS
SHOOT

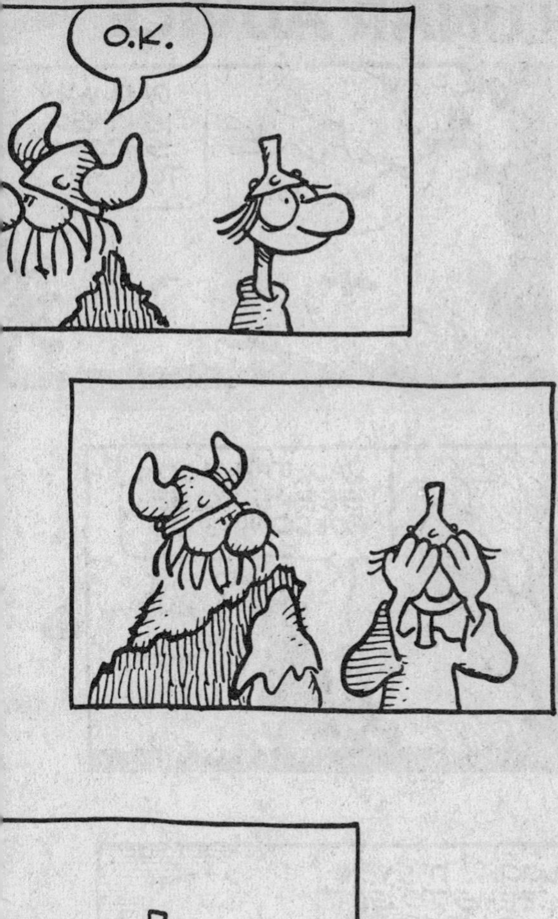
O.K.
DIK BROWNE
12-1

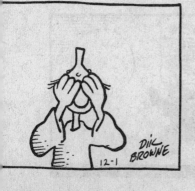

LUNAR ADVICE

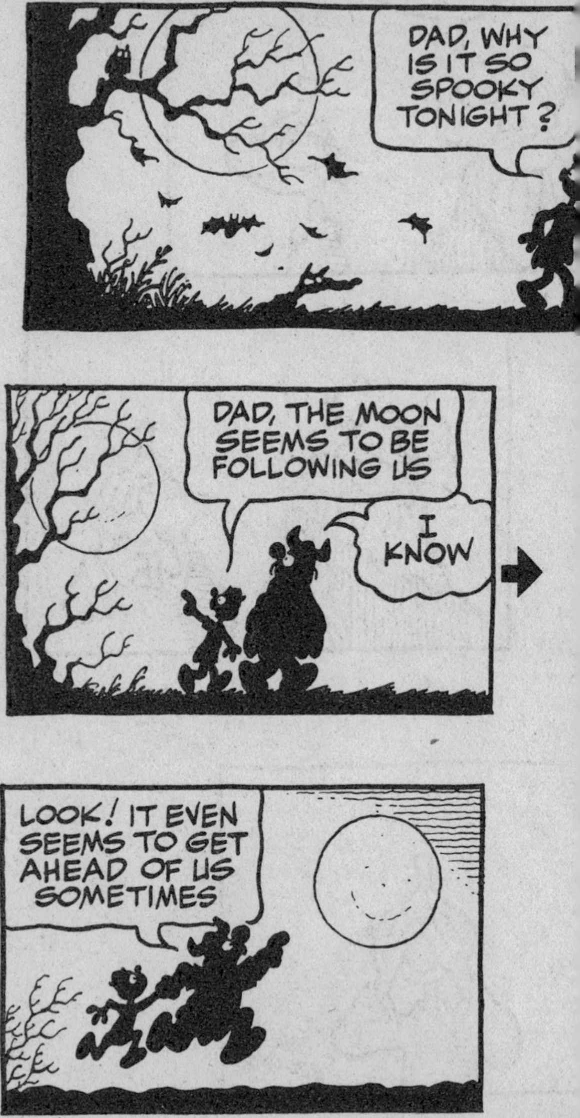
DAD, WHY IS IT SO SPOOKY TONIGHT?
DAD, THE MOON SEEMS TO BE FOLLOWING US
I KNOW
LOOK! IT EVEN SEEMS TO GET AHEAD OF US SOMETIMES

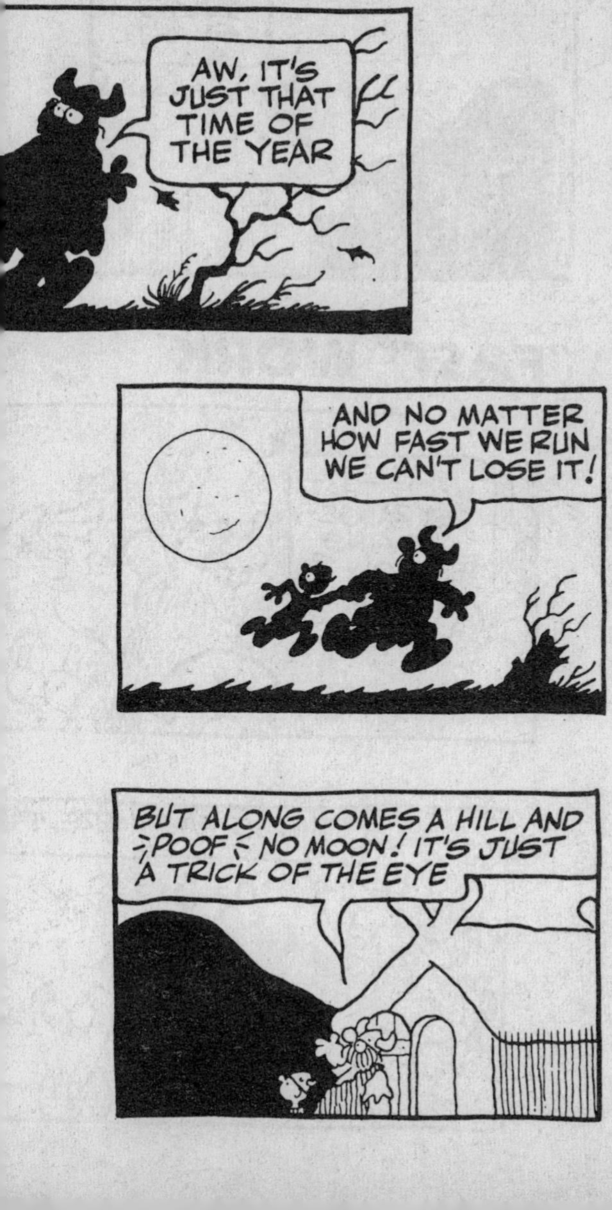
AW, IT'S JUST THAT TIME OF THE YEAR
AND NO MATTER HOW FAST WE RUN WE CAN'T LOSE IT!
BUT ALONG COMES A HILL AND POOF NO MOON! IT'S JUST A TRICK OF THE EYE

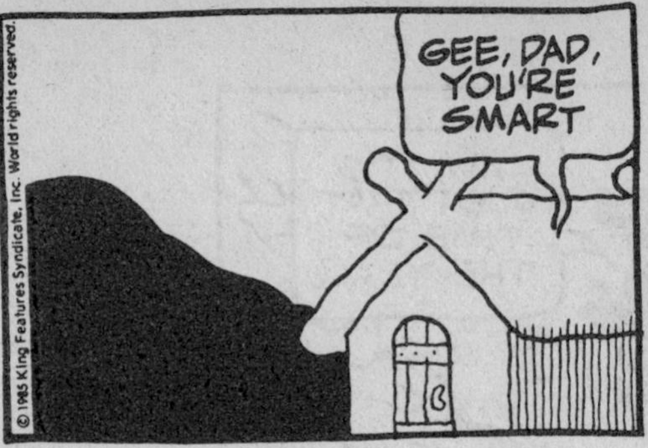
© 1985 King Features Syndicate, Inc. World rights reserved.
GEE, DAD, YOU'RE SMART

"FAST" WORK

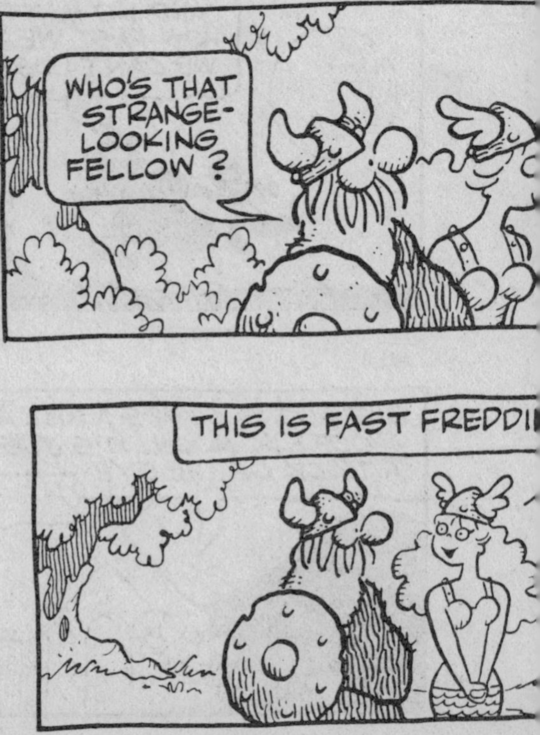
WHO'S THAT STRANGE-LOOKING FELLOW ?
THIS IS FAST FREDDI

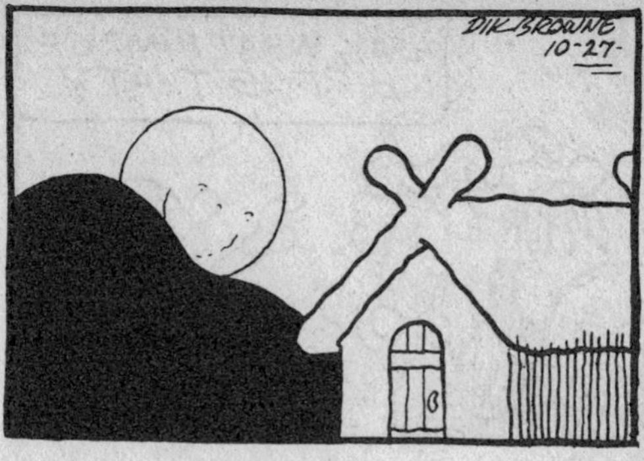
DIK BROWNE
10-27-

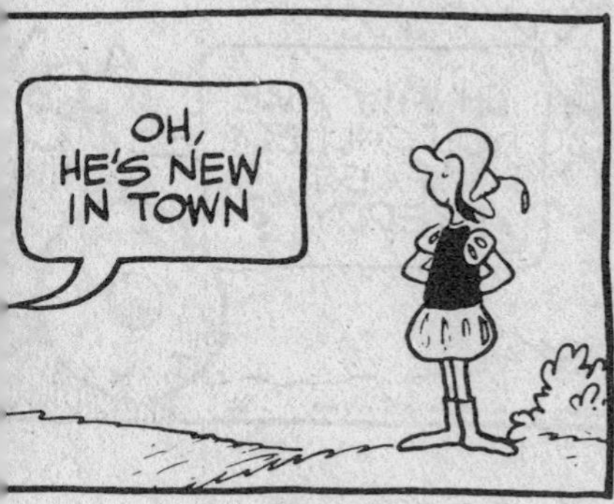
OH, HE'S NEW IN TOWN

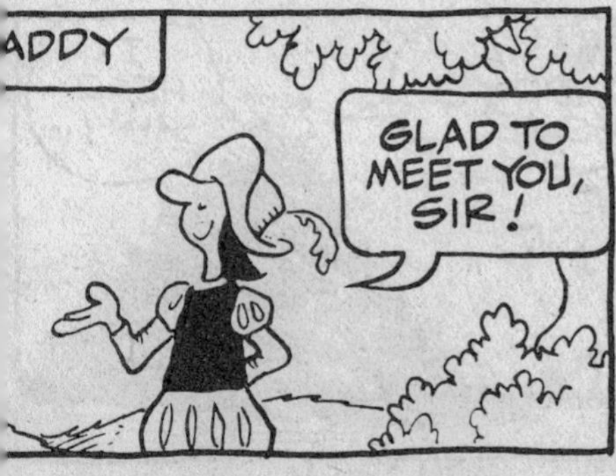
ADDY
GLAD TO MEET YOU, SIR!

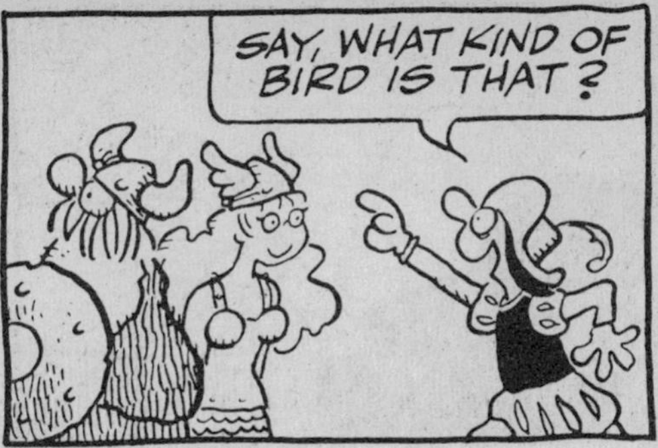
SAY, WHAT KIND OF BIRD IS THAT?

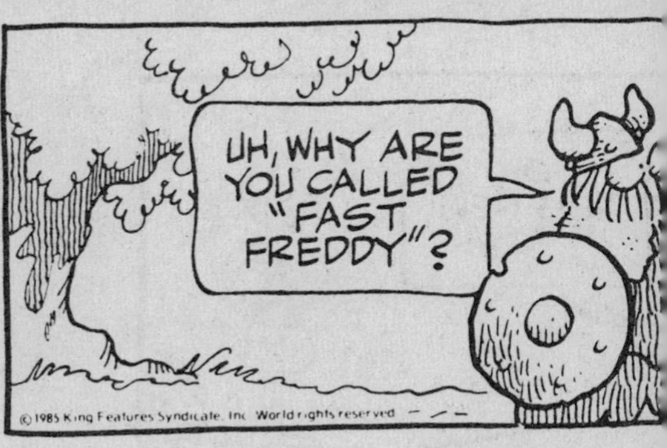
UH, WHY ARE YOU CALLED "FAST FREDDY"?
© 1985 King Features Syndicate, Inc. World rights reserved

KILL-JOY

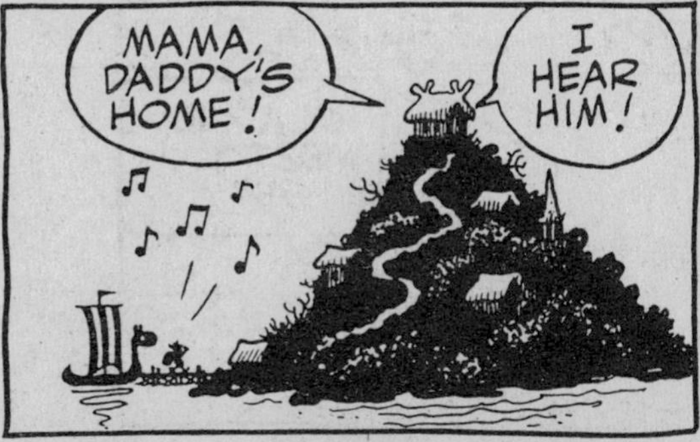
MAMA, DADDY'S HOME!
I HEAR HIM!

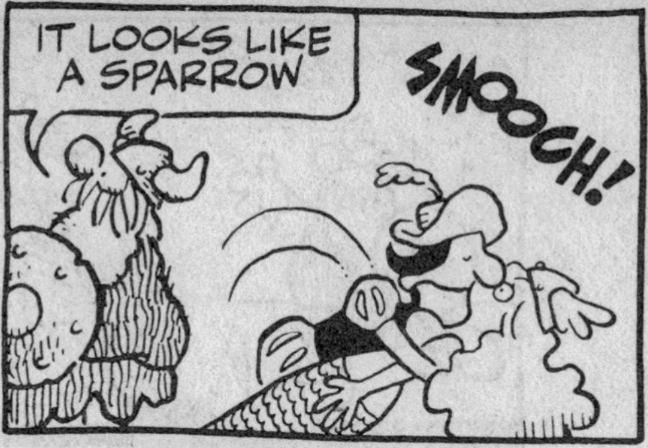
IT LOOKS LIKE A SPARROW
SMOOCH!

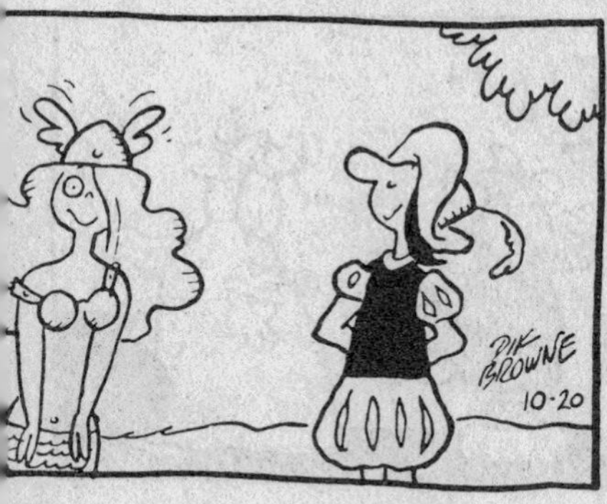
DIK BROWNE
10-20

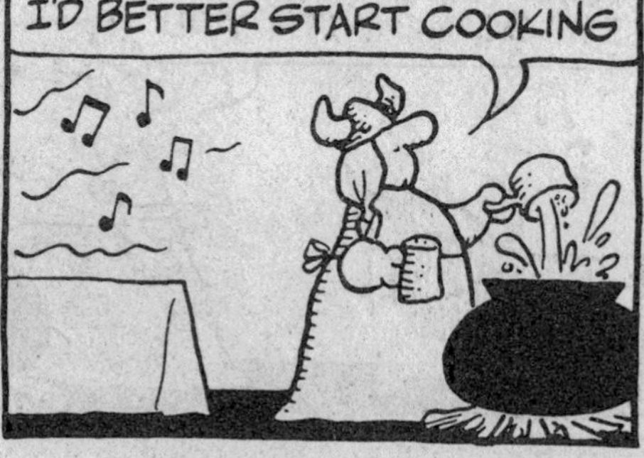
I'D BETTER START COOKING

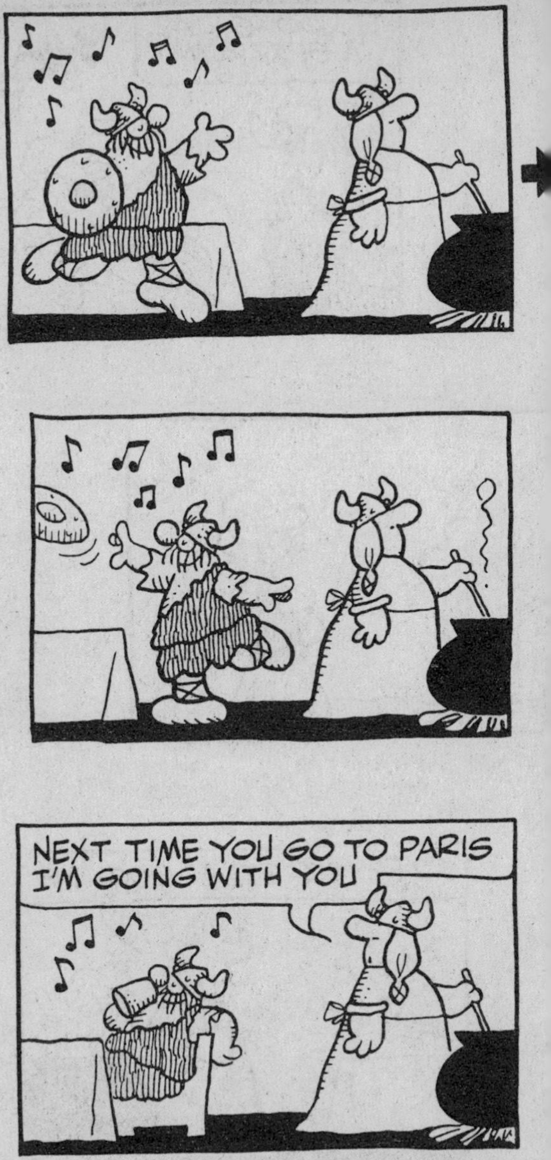
NEXT TIME YOU GO TO PARIS I'M GOING WITH YOU

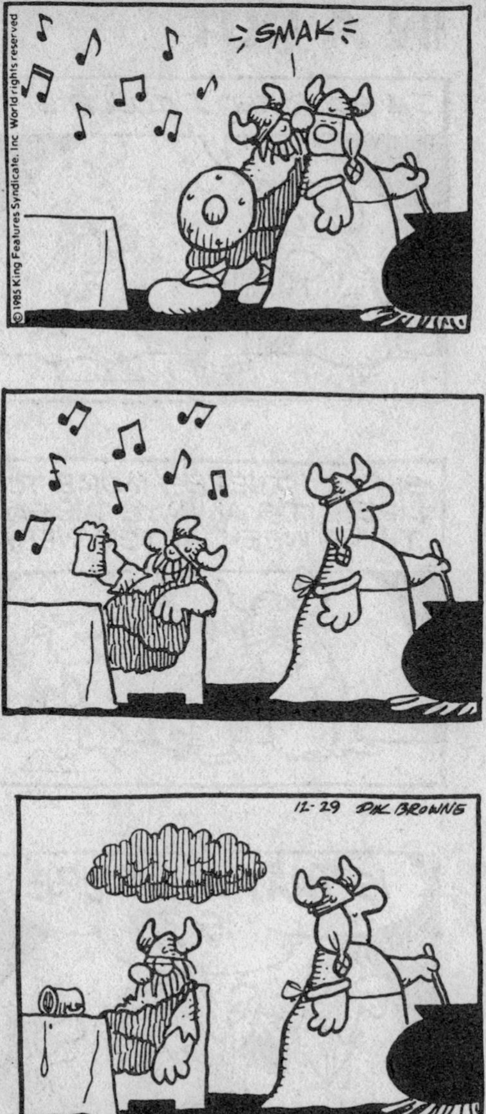
SMAK
12-29 DIK BROWNE

IN A RUT

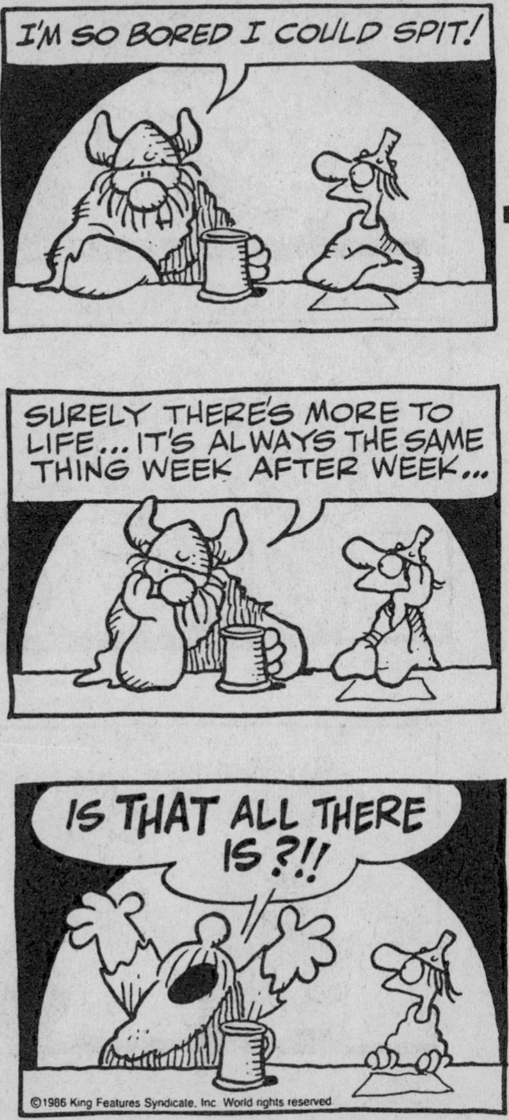

I'M SO BORED I COULD SPIT!
SURELY THERE'S MORE TO LIFE... IT'S ALWAYS THE SAME THING WEEK AFTER WEEK...
IS THAT ALL THERE IS ?!!
©1986 King Features Syndicate, Inc World rights reserved

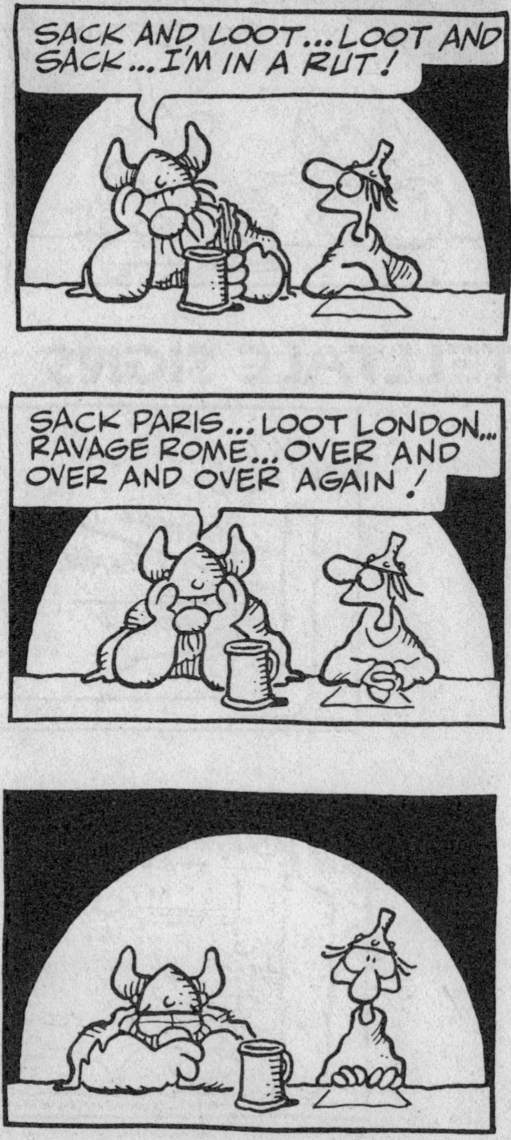
SACK AND LOOT...LOOT AND SACK...I'M IN A RUT!
SACK PARIS...LOOT LONDON... RAVAGE ROME...OVER AND OVER AND OVER AGAIN!

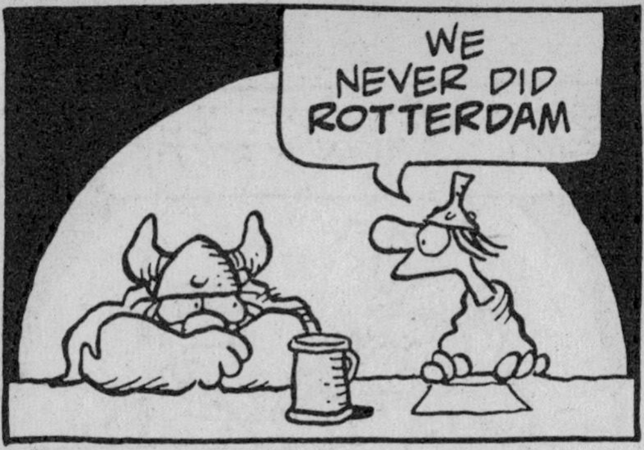
WE NEVER DID ROTTERDAM

TELLTALE SIGNS

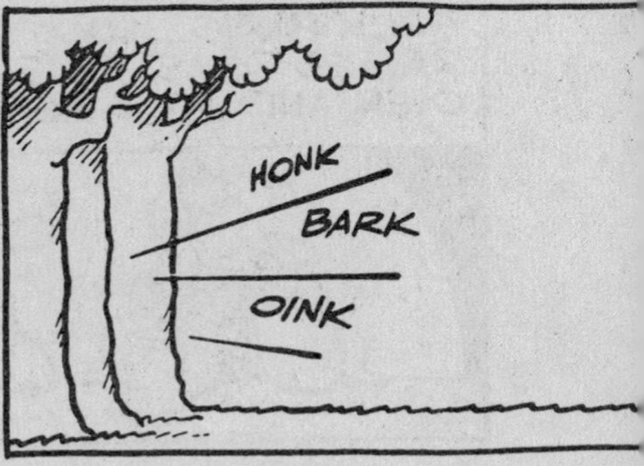
HONK
BARK
OINK

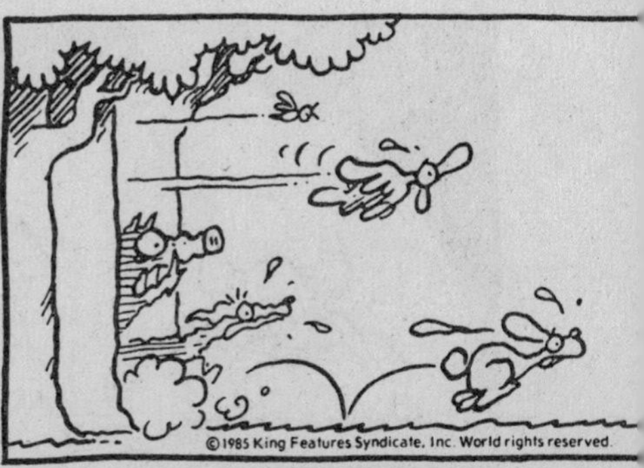
©1985 King Features Syndicate, Inc. World rights reserved.

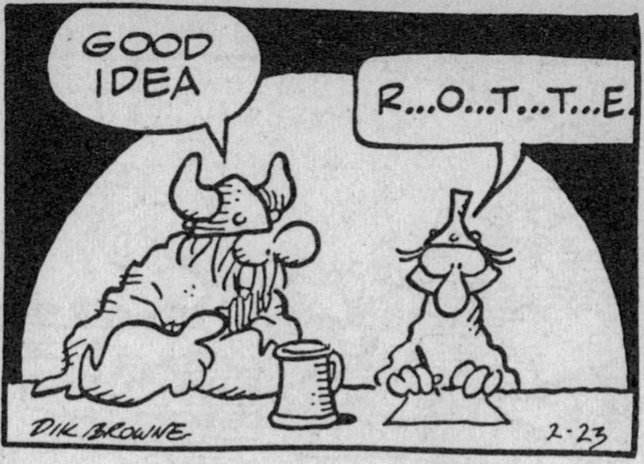
GOOD IDEA
R...O...T...T...E.
DIK BROWNE
2-23

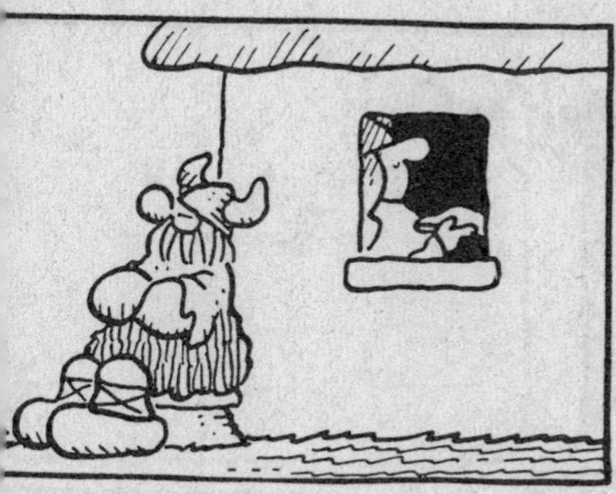

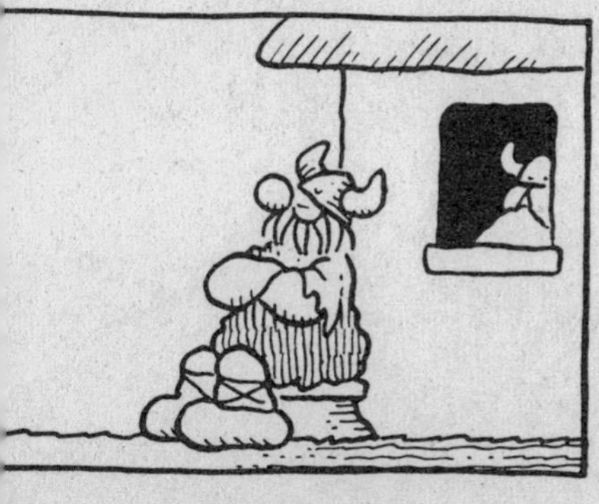

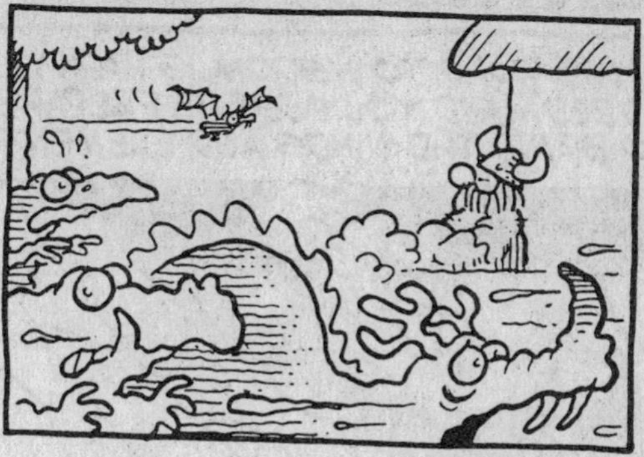

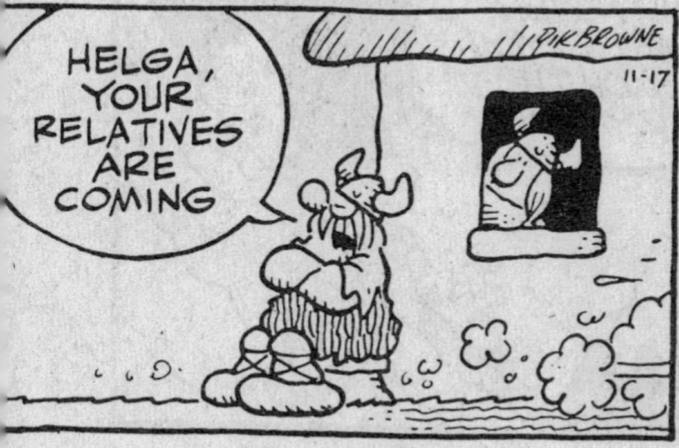
HELGA, YOUR RELATIVES ARE COMING
DIK BROWNE
11-17

ZENITH

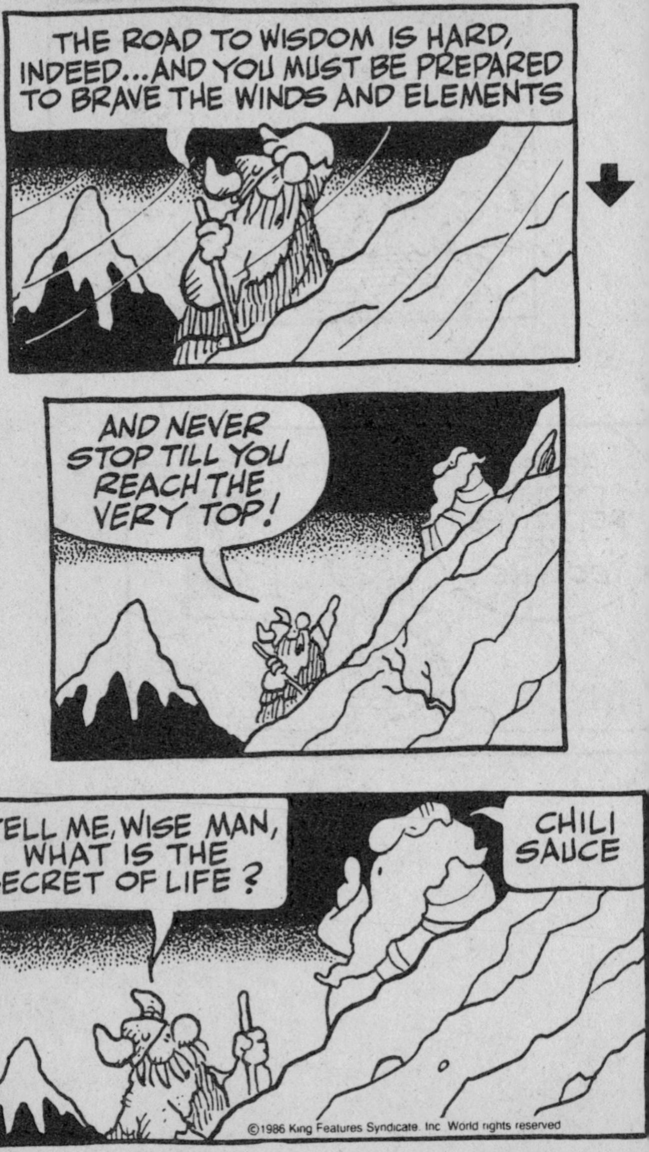

THE ROAD TO WISDOM IS HARD, INDEED...AND YOU MUST BE PREPARED TO BRAVE THE WINDS AND ELEMENTS
AND NEVER STOP TILL YOU REACH THE VERY TOP!
TELL ME, WISE MAN, WHAT IS THE SECRET OF LIFE ?
CHILI SAUCE
©1986 King Features Syndicate, Inc. World rights reserved

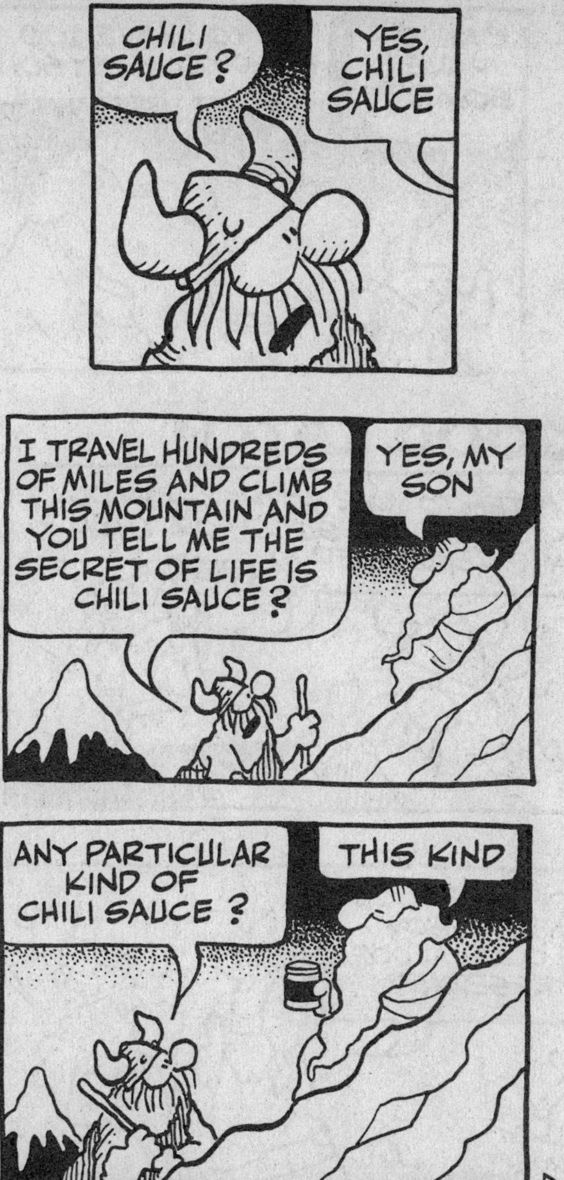
CHILI SAUCE?
YES, CHILI SAUCE
I TRAVEL HUNDREDS OF MILES AND CLIMB THIS MOUNTAIN AND YOU TELL ME THE SECRET OF LIFE IS CHILI SAUCE?
YES, MY SON
ANY PARTICULAR KIND OF CHILI SAUCE?
THIS KIND

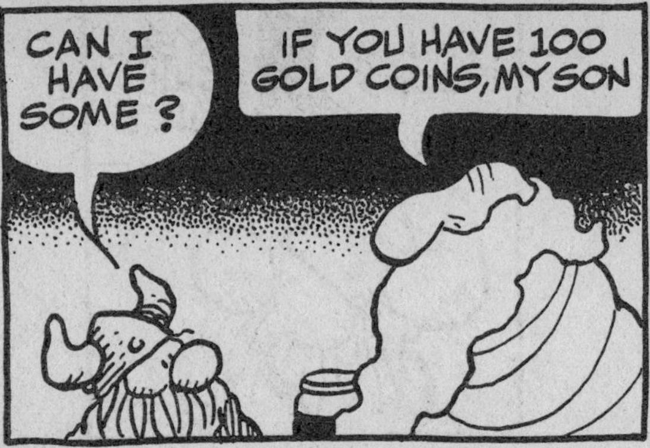
CAN I HAVE SOME ?
IF YOU HAVE 100 GOLD COINS, MY SON

GOOD CATCH

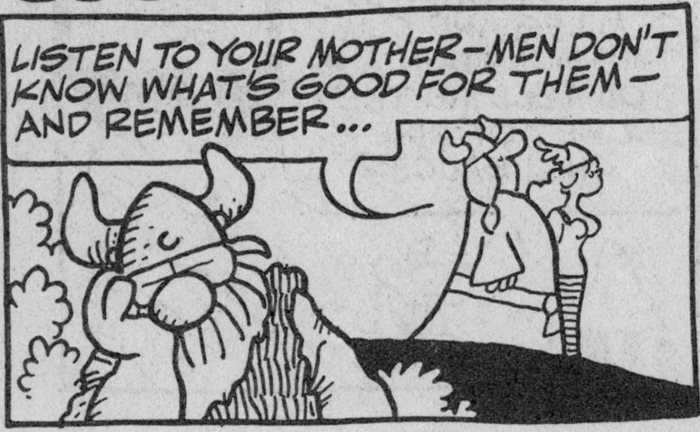
LISTEN TO YOUR MOTHER—MEN DON'T KNOW WHAT'S GOOD FOR THEM—AND REMEMBER...

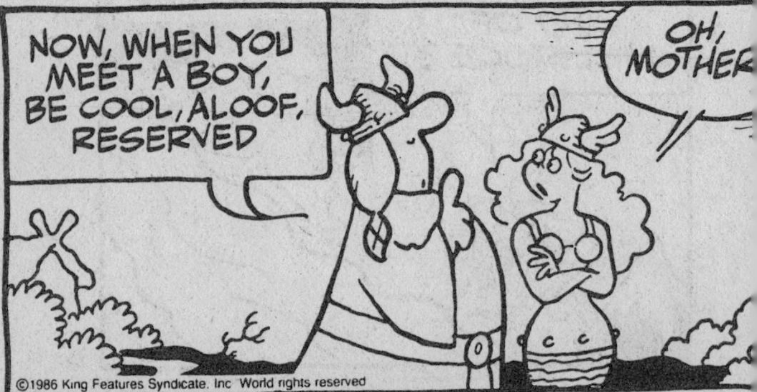
NOW, WHEN YOU MEET A BOY, BE COOL, ALOOF, RESERVED
OH, MOTHE

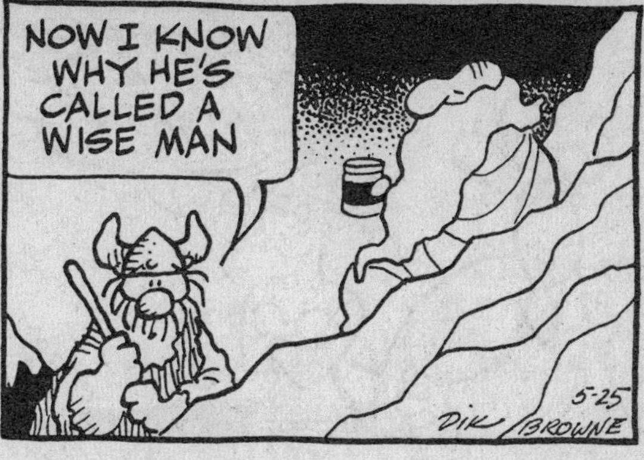
NOW I KNOW WHY HE'S CALLED A WISE MAN
5-25
DIK BROWNE

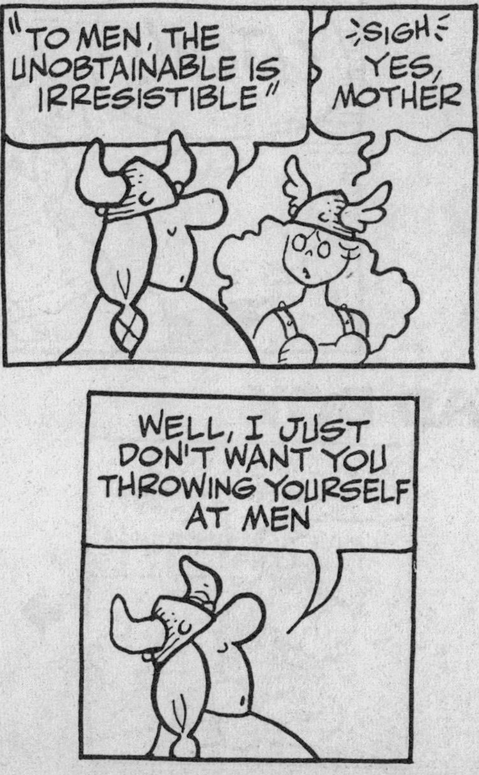
"TO MEN, THE UNOBTAINABLE IS IRRESISTIBLE"
SIGH YES, MOTHER
WELL, I JUST DON'T WANT YOU THROWING YOURSELF AT MEN

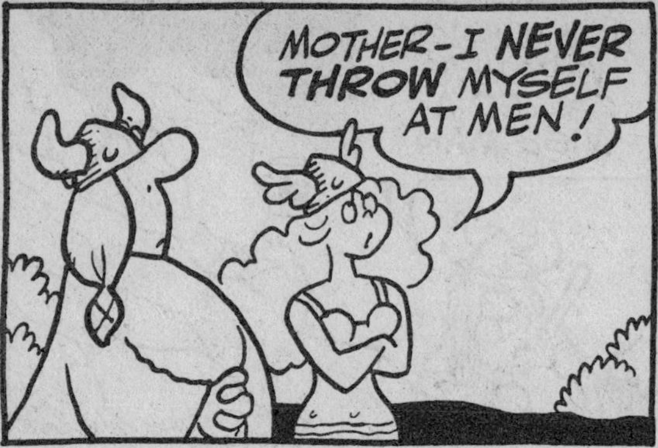
MOTHER- I NEVER THROW MYSELF AT MEN!

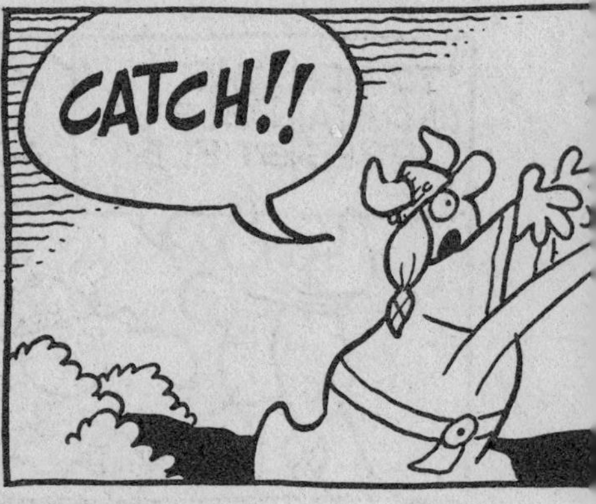
CATCH!!

BAD BOY

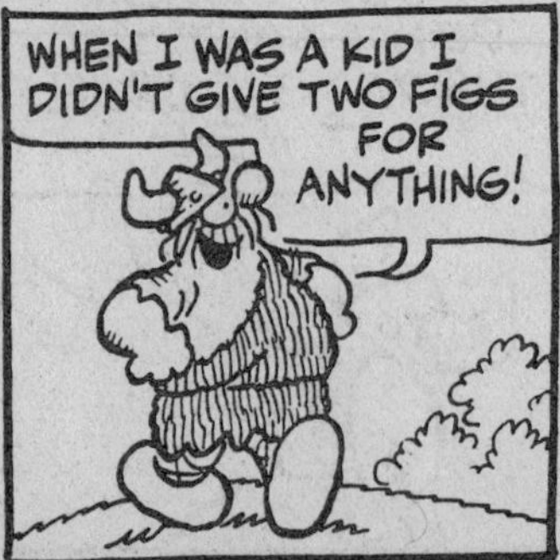
WHEN I WAS A KID I DIDN'T GIVE TWO FIGS FOR ANYTHING!

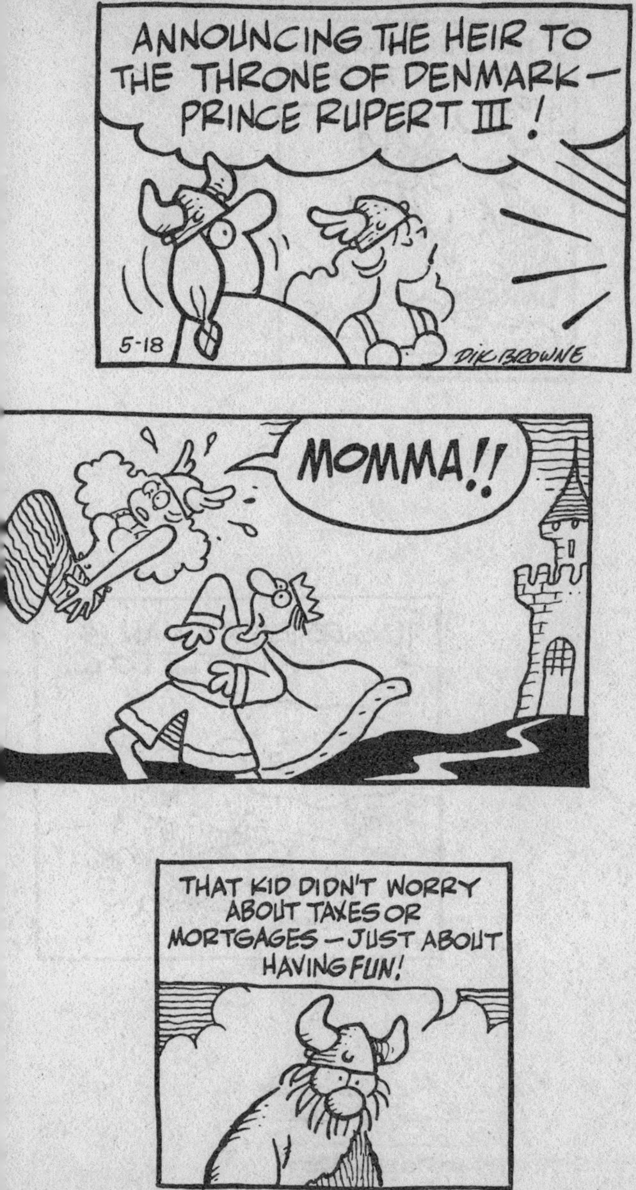
ANNOUNCING THE HEIR TO THE THRONE OF DENMARK— PRINCE RUPERT III !
5-18
DIK BROWNE
MOMMA!!
THAT KID DIDN'T WORRY ABOUT TAXES OR MORTGAGES—JUST ABOUT HAVING FUN!

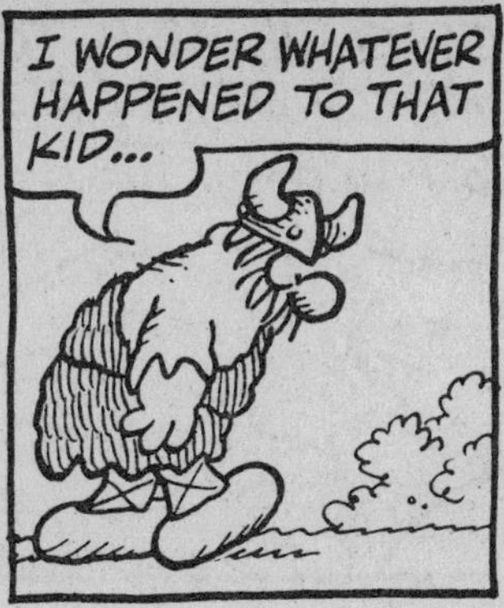
I WONDER WHATEVER HAPPENED TO THAT KID...

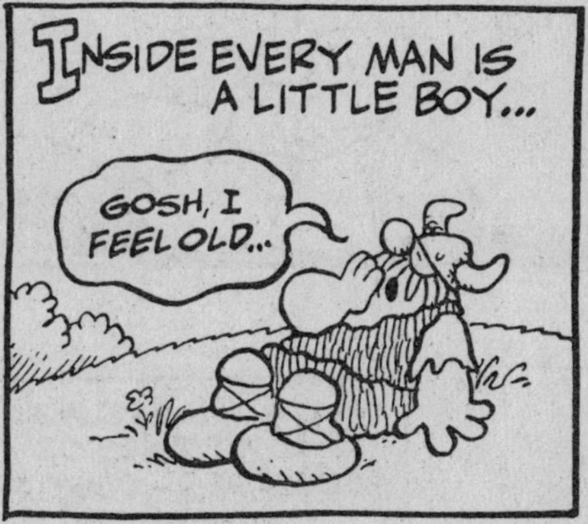
INSIDE EVERY MAN IS A LITTLE BOY...
GOSH, I FEEL OLD...

TRYING TO GET OUT!

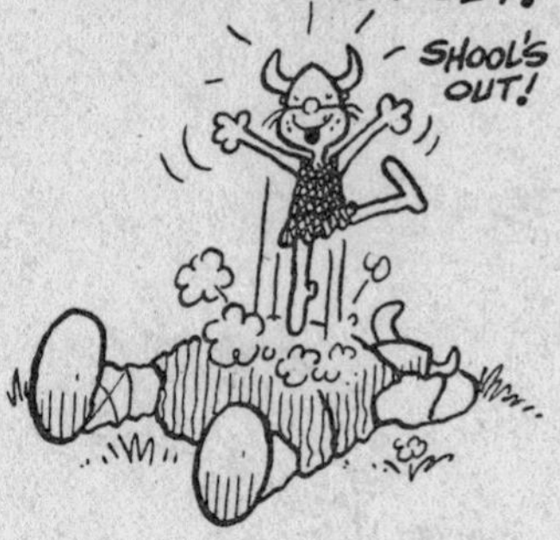
SHOOL'S OUT!

A *MEAN* LITTLE BOY

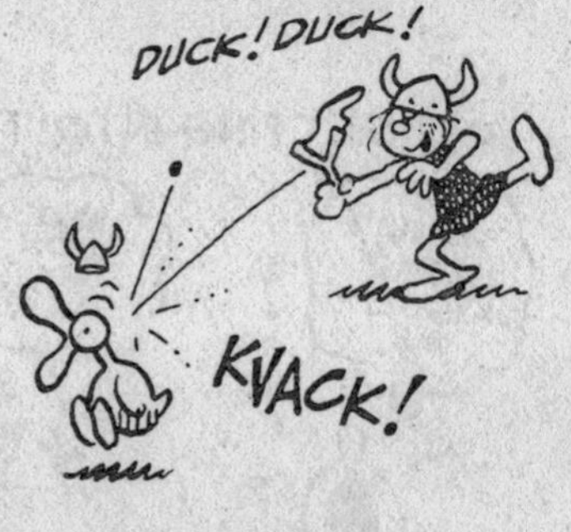
DUCK! DUCK!
KVACK!

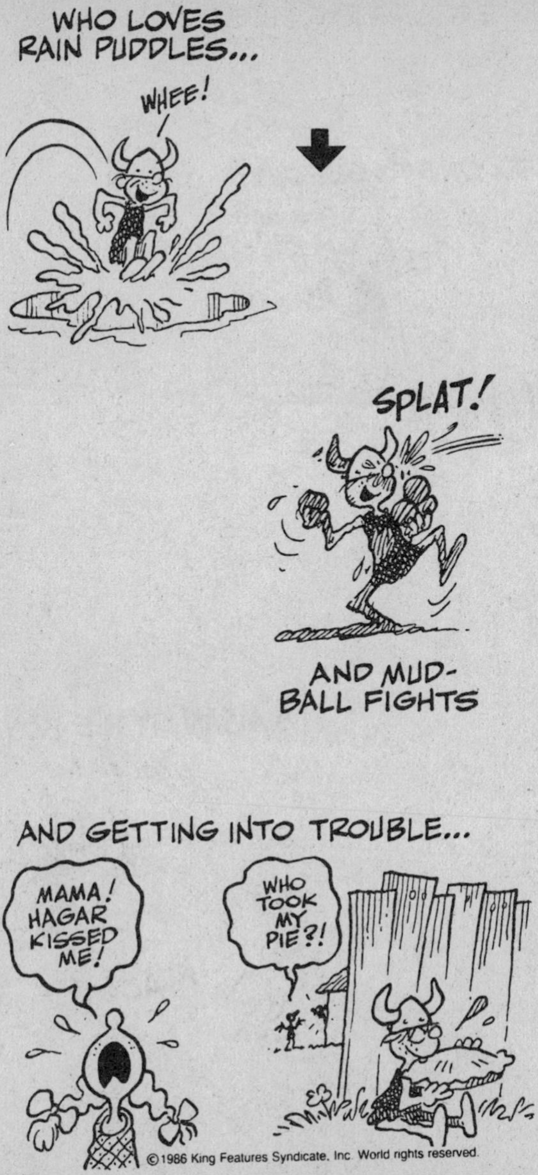
WHO LOVES RAIN PUDDLES...
WHEE!
SPLAT!
AND MUD-BALL FIGHTS
AND GETTING INTO TROUBLE...
MAMA! HAGAR KISSED ME!
WHO TOOK MY PIE?!

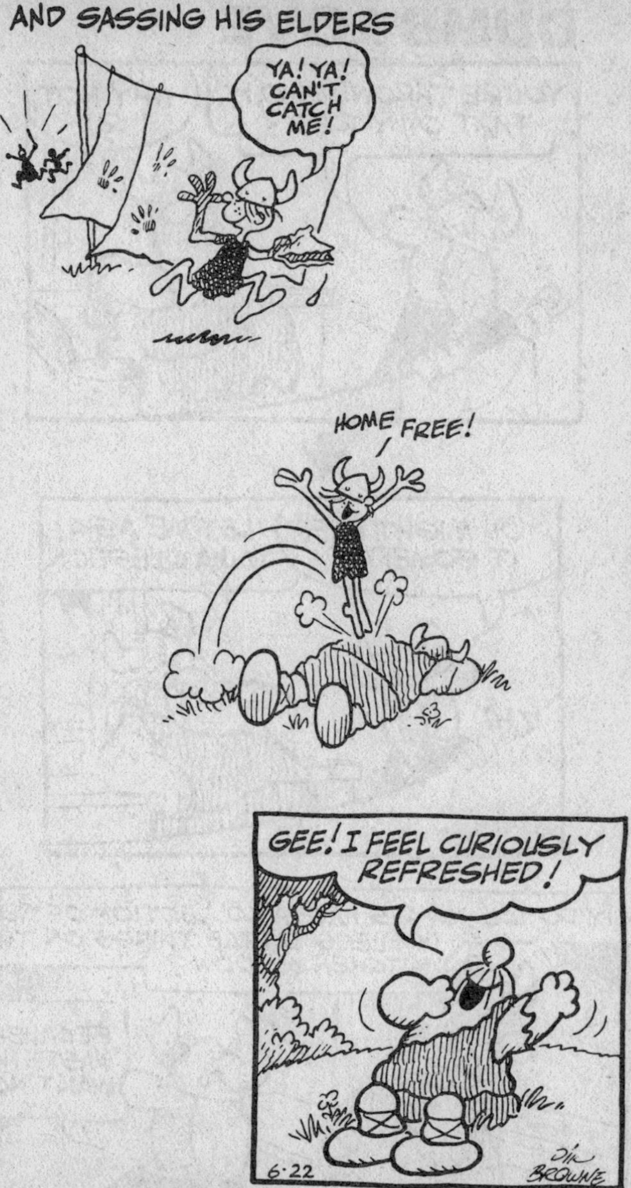
AND SASSING HIS ELDERS
YA! YA! CAN'T CATCH ME!
HOME FREE!
GEE! I FEEL CURIOUSLY REFRESHED!
6·22
DIK BROWNE

DUMB LOVE

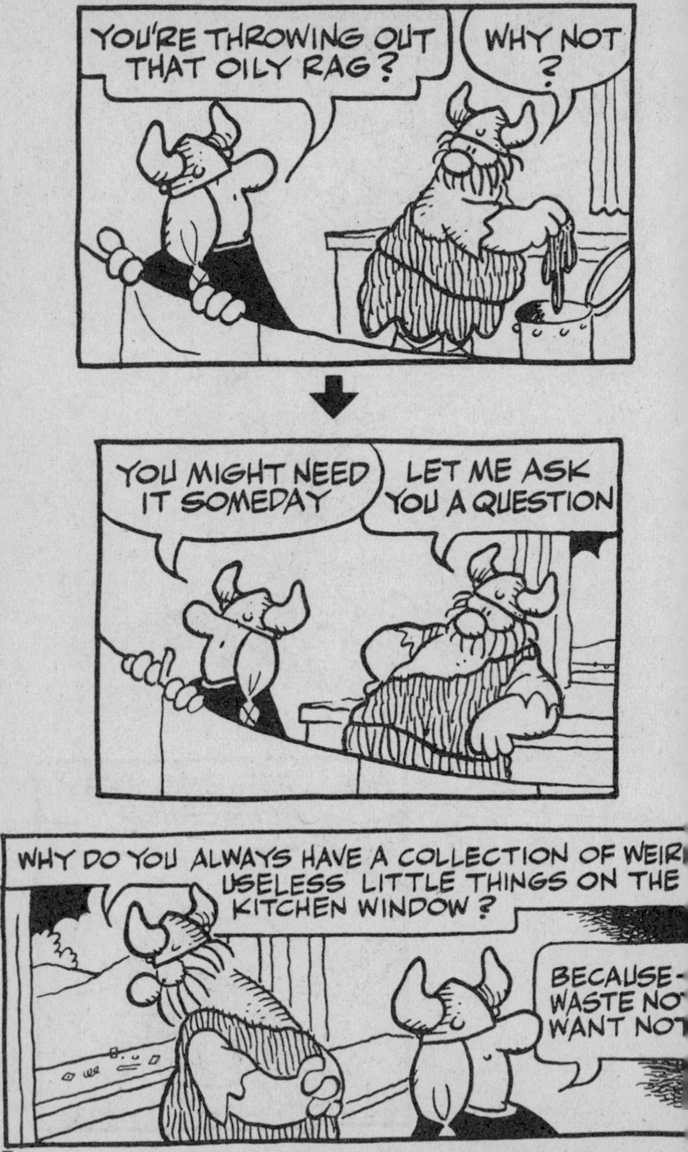
YOU'RE THROWING OUT THAT OILY RAG?
WHY NOT?
YOU MIGHT NEED IT SOMEDAY
LET ME ASK YOU A QUESTION
WHY DO YOU ALWAYS HAVE A COLLECTION OF WEIR USELESS LITTLE THINGS ON THE KITCHEN WINDOW?
BECAUSE- WASTE NO WANT NO

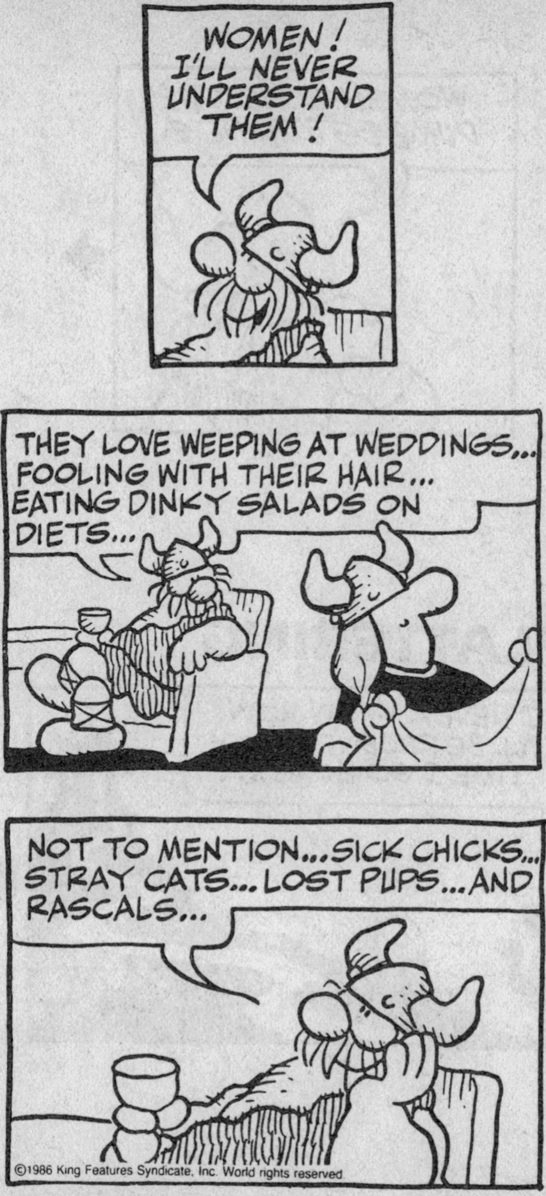
WOMEN! I'LL NEVER UNDERSTAND THEM!
THEY LOVE WEEPING AT WEDDINGS... FOOLING WITH THEIR HAIR... EATING DINKY SALADS ON DIETS...
NOT TO MENTION...SICK CHICKS... STRAY CATS...LOST PUPS...AND RASCALS...
©1986 King Features Syndicate, Inc. World rights reserved

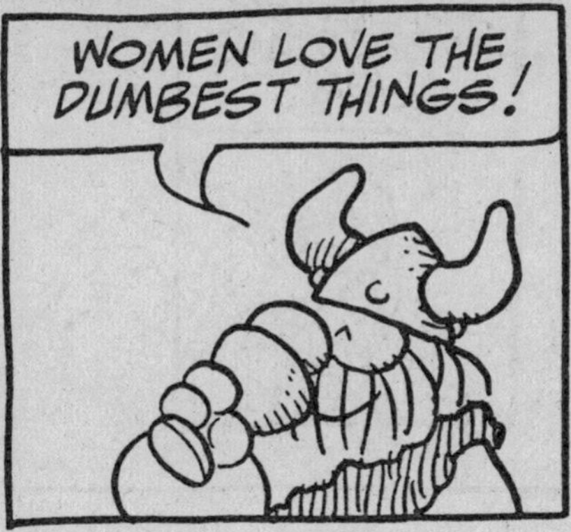
WOMEN LOVE THE DUMBEST THINGS!

FLATTERING

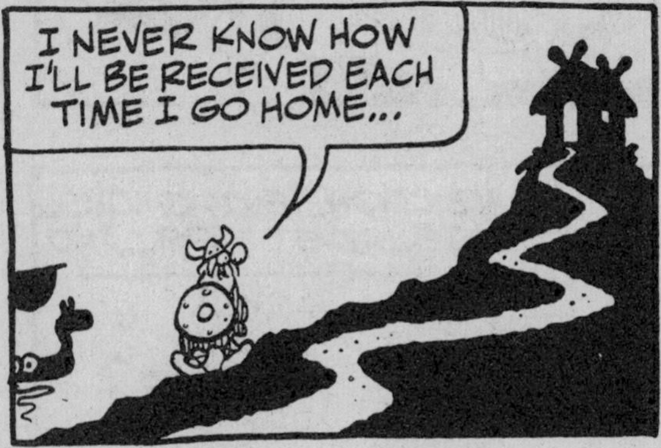
I NEVER KNOW HOW I'LL BE RECEIVED EACH TIME I GO HOME...

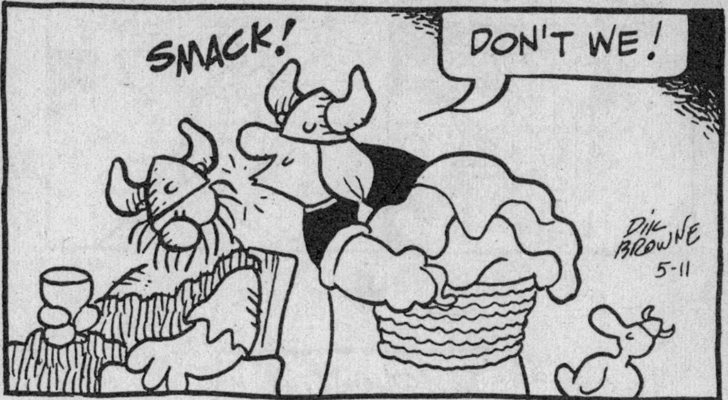
SMACK!
DON'T WE!
DIK BROWNE
5-11

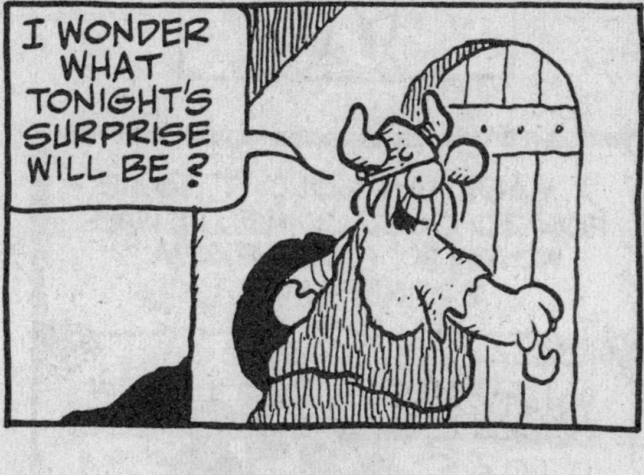
I WONDER WHAT TONIGHT'S SURPRISE WILL BE ?

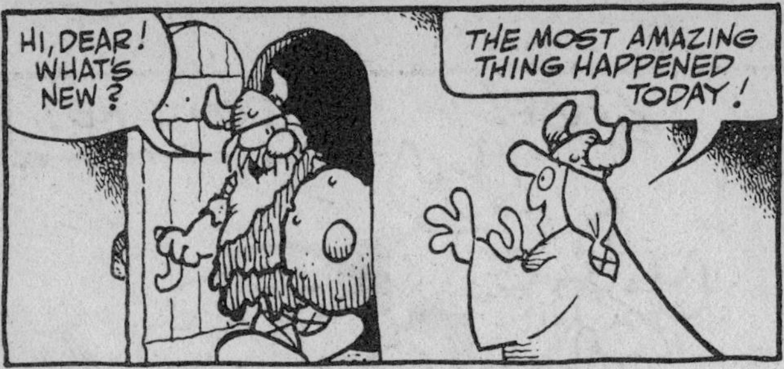
HI, DEAR! WHAT'S NEW?
THE MOST AMAZING THING HAPPENED TODAY!

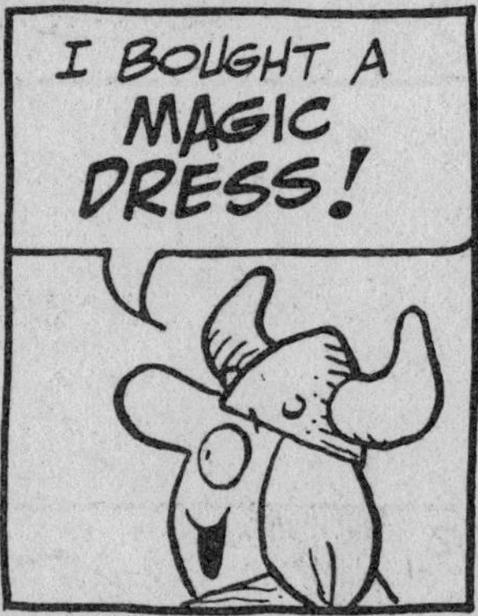
I BOUGHT A MAGIC DRESS!

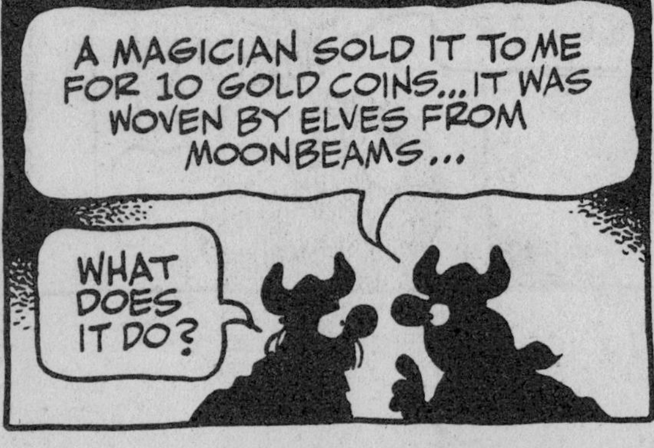
A MAGICIAN SOLD IT TO ME FOR 10 GOLD COINS... IT WAS WOVEN BY ELVES FROM MOONBEAMS...
WHAT DOES IT DO?

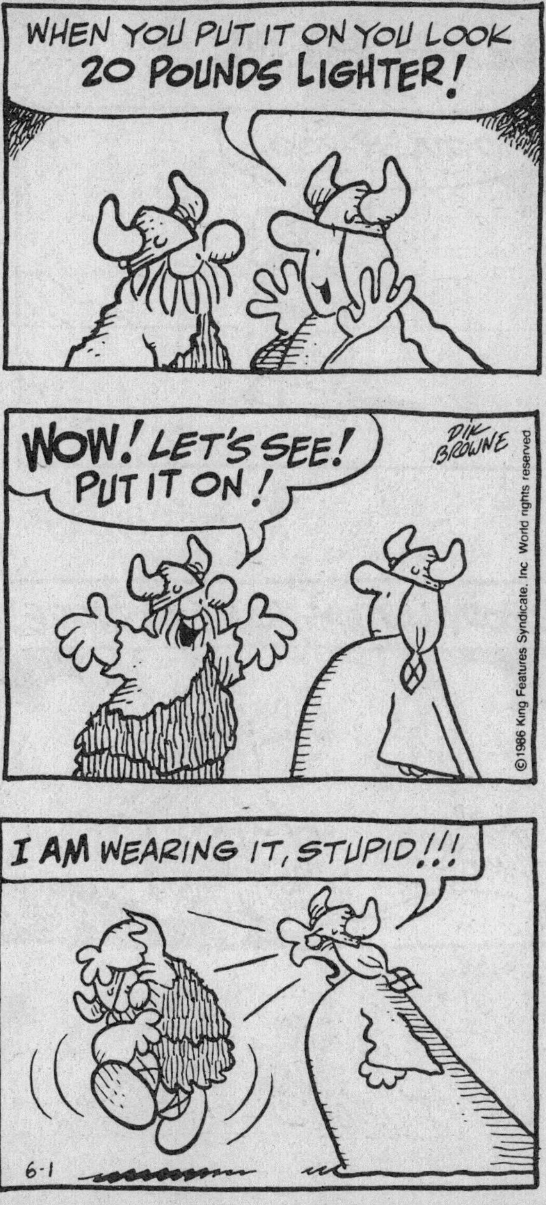
WHEN YOU PUT IT ON YOU LOOK 20 POUNDS LIGHTER!
WOW! LET'S SEE! PUT IT ON!
DIK BROWNE
©1986 King Features Syndicate, Inc World rights reserved
I AM WEARING IT, STUPID!!!
6-1

HEAR HERE

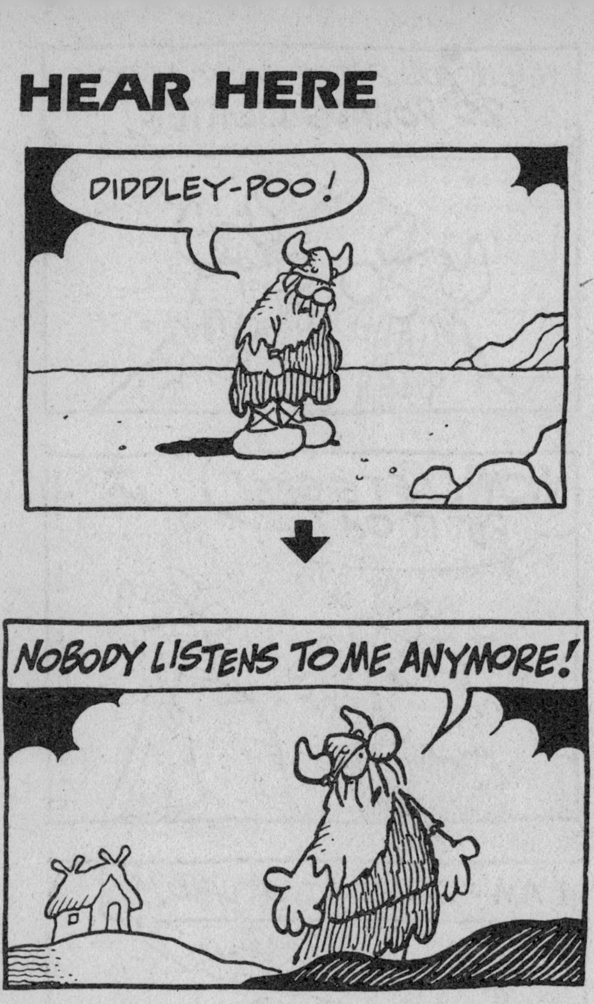
DIDDLEY-POO!
NOBODY LISTENS TO ME ANYMORE!

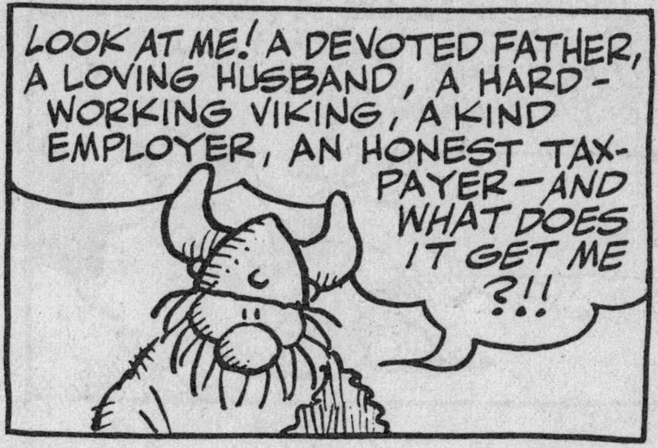
LOOK AT ME! A DEVOTED FATHER, A LOVING HUSBAND, A HARD-WORKING VIKING, A KIND EMPLOYER, AN HONEST TAX-PAYER—AND WHAT DOES IT GET ME ?!!

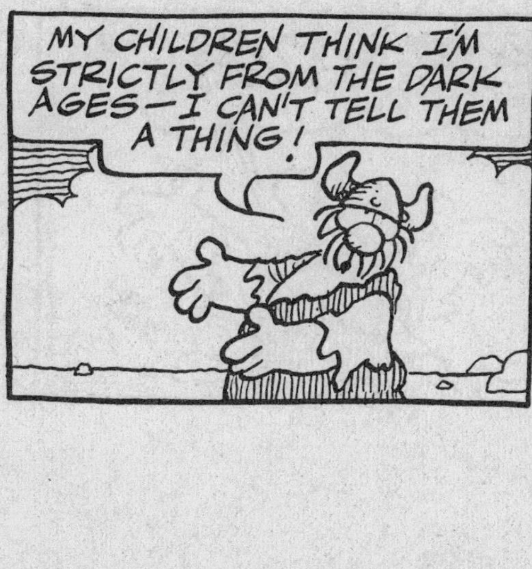
MY CHILDREN THINK I'M STRICTLY FROM THE DARK AGES—I CAN'T TELL THEM A THING!

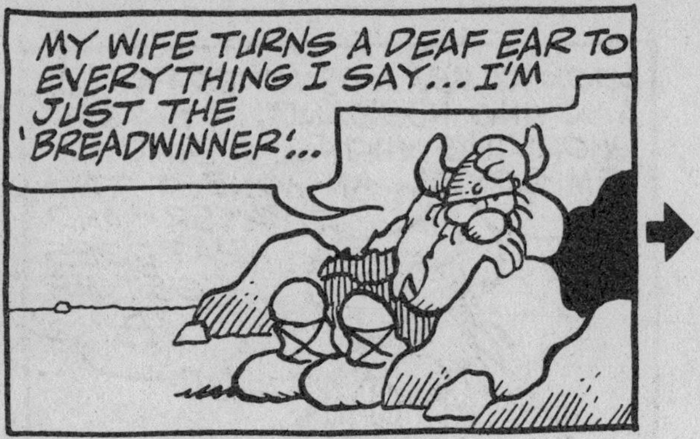
MY WIFE TURNS A DEAF EAR TO EVERYTHING I SAY... I'M JUST THE 'BREADWINNER'!...

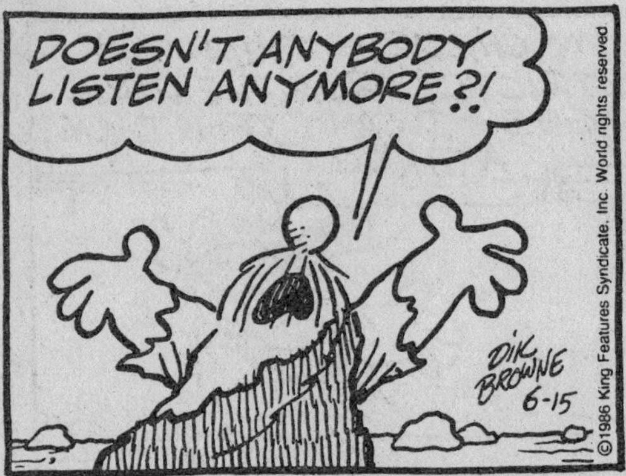
DOESN'T ANYBODY LISTEN ANYMORE?!
DIK BROWNE 6-15
©1986 King Features Syndicate, Inc. World rights reserved

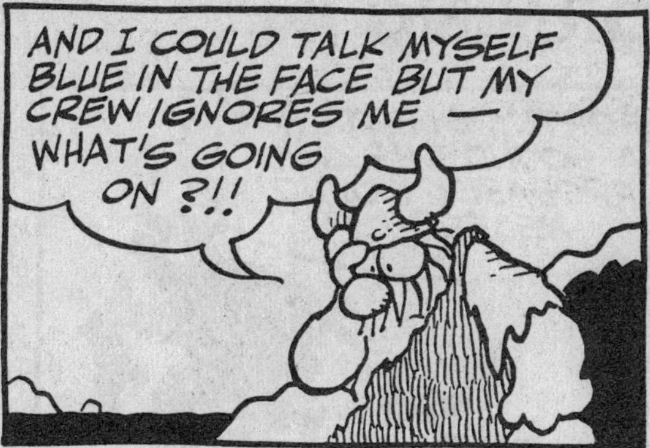
AND I COULD TALK MYSELF BLUE IN THE FACE BUT MY CREW IGNORES ME — WHAT'S GOING ON ?!!

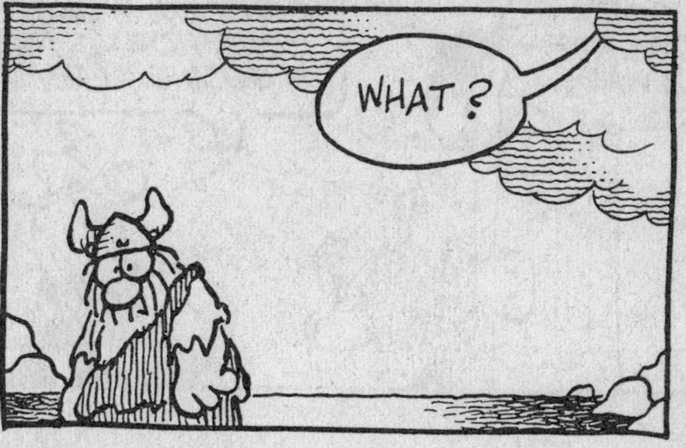
WHAT ?

HORNING IN

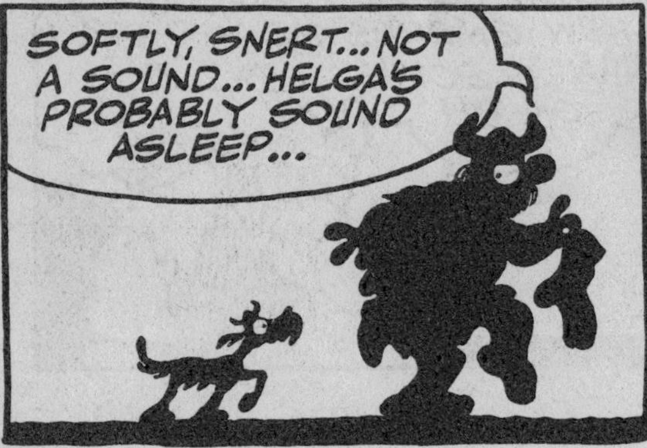
SOFTLY, SNERT... NOT A SOUND... HELGA'S PROBABLY SOUND ASLEEP...

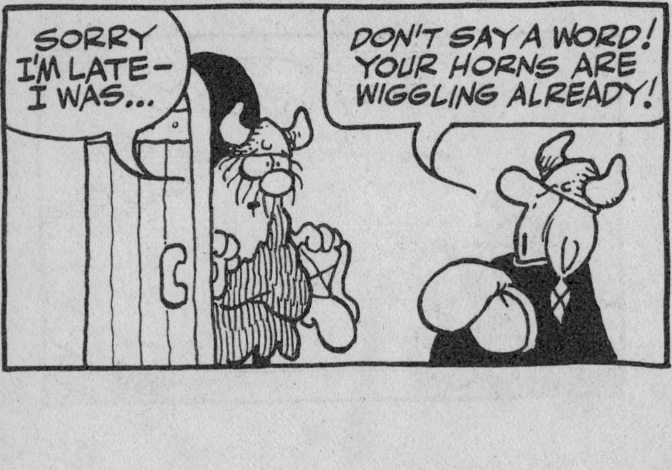
SORRY I'M LATE- I WAS...
DON'T SAY A WORD! YOUR HORNS ARE WIGGLING ALREADY!

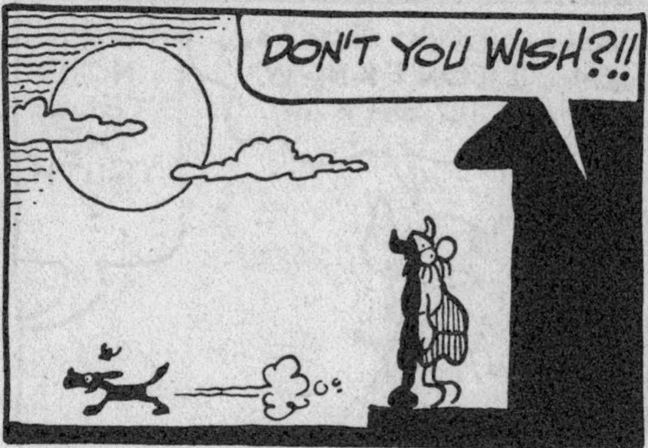
DON'T YOU WISH?!!

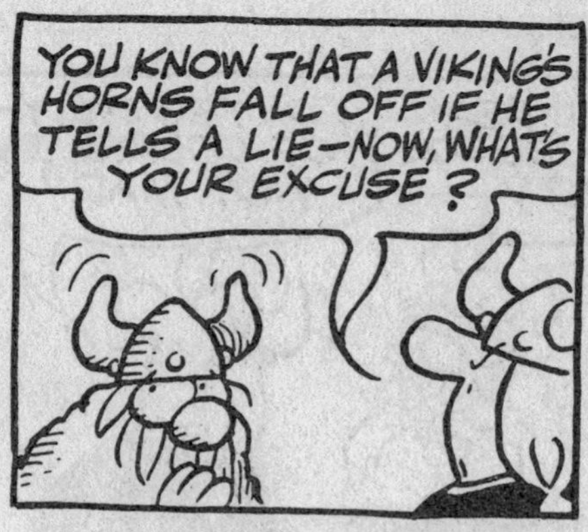
YOU KNOW THAT A VIKING'S HORNS FALL OFF IF HE TELLS A LIE—NOW, WHAT'S YOUR EXCUSE?

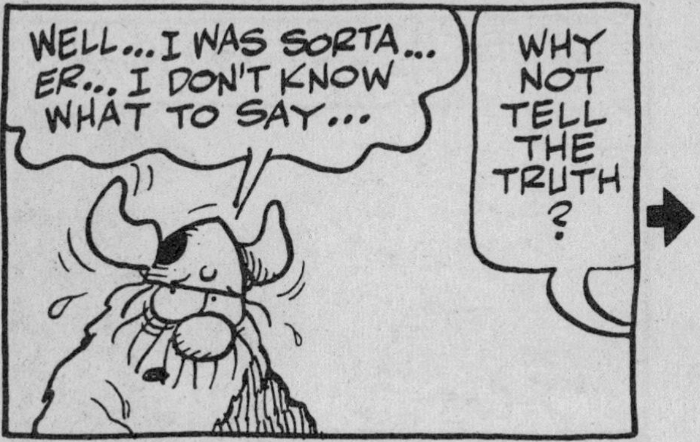
WELL...I WAS SORTA... ER... I DON'T KNOW WHAT TO SAY...
WHY NOT TELL THE TRUTH?

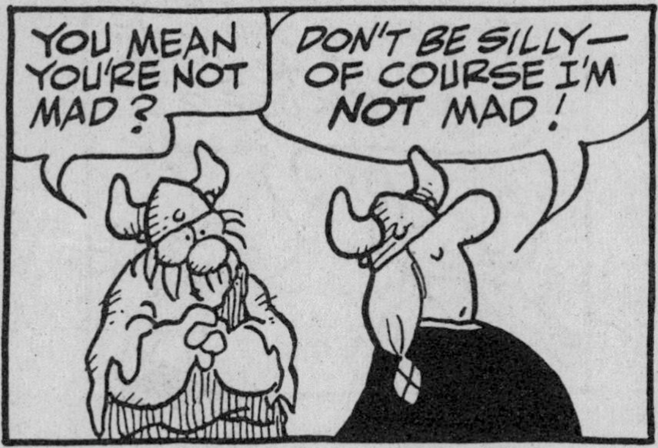
YOU MEAN YOU'RE NOT MAD?
DON'T BE SILLY— OF COURSE I'M NOT MAD!

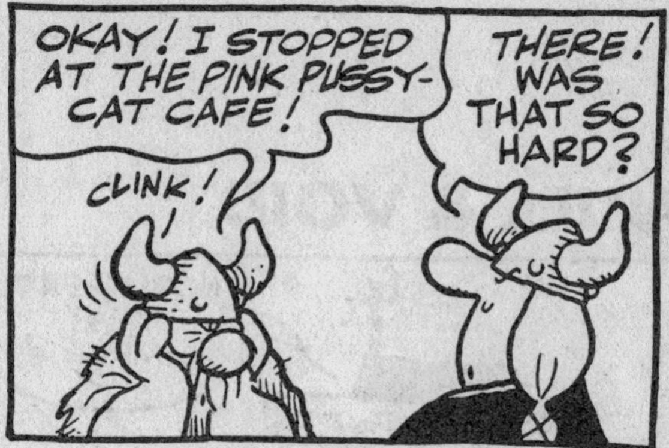
OKAY! I STOPPED AT THE PINK PUSSY-CAT CAFE!
CLINK!
THERE! WAS THAT SO HARD?

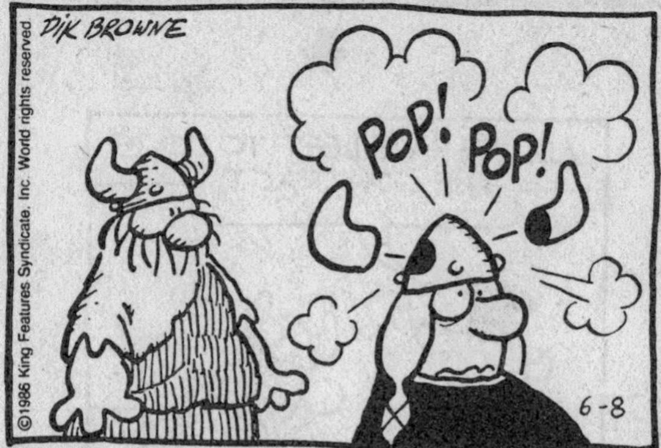
DIK BROWNE
POP! POP!
6-8
©1986 King Features Syndicate, Inc. World rights reserved.

NULL & VOID

NOW, WASN'T THAT SIMPLE?
KOYER THE LAWYER
TALK IS CHEAP
PLEA BARGAIN!
FREE ADVICE
ALL WE HAVE LEFT TO DO IS THE CONTRACT

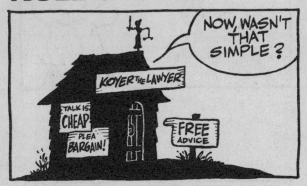

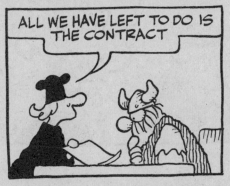

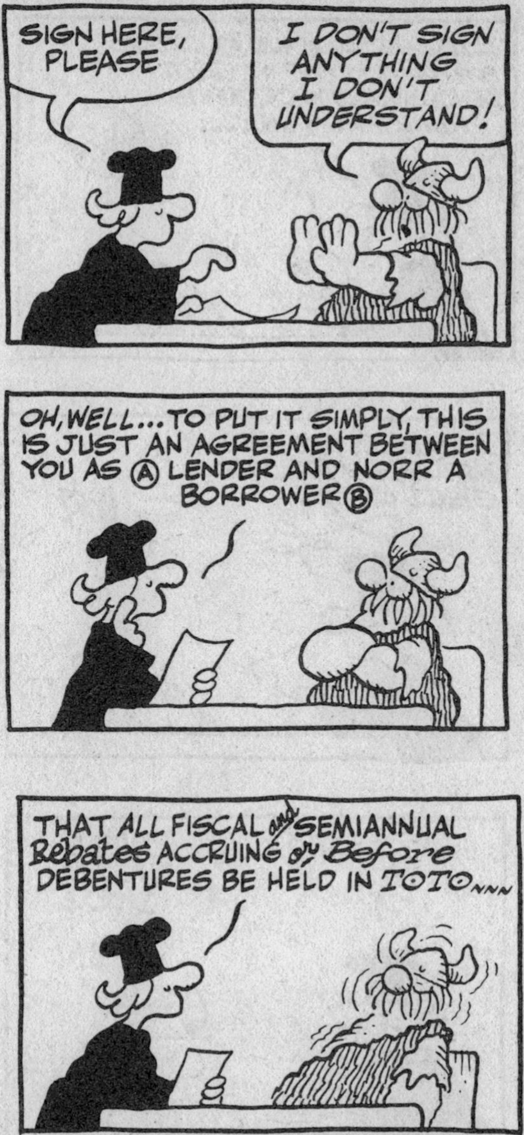
SIGN HERE, PLEASE
I DON'T SIGN ANYTHING I DON'T UNDERSTAND!
OH, WELL... TO PUT IT SIMPLY, THIS IS JUST AN AGREEMENT BETWEEN YOU AS Ⓐ LENDER AND NORR A BORROWER Ⓑ
THAT ALL FISCAL and SEMIANNUAL Rebates ACCRUING or Before DEBENTURES BE HELD IN TOTOnnn

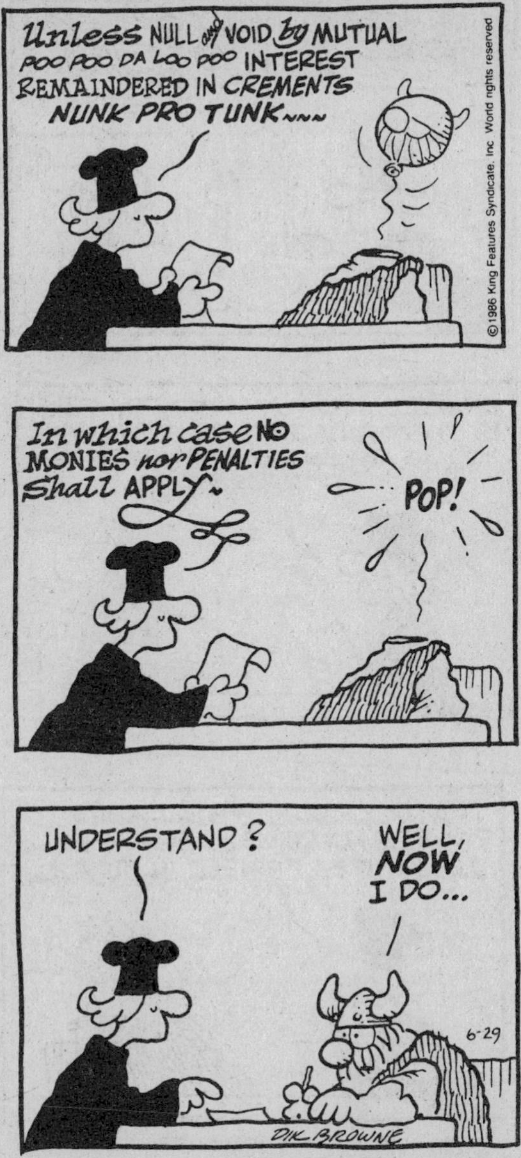
Unless NULL VOID by MUTUAL
POO POO DA LOO POO INTEREST
REMAINDERED IN CREMENTS
NUNK PRO TUNK~~~
© 1986 King Features Syndicate, Inc. World rights reserved
In which case NO
MONIES nor PENALTIES
Shall APPLY~
POP!
UNDERSTAND?
WELL, NOW I DO...
6-29
DIK BROWNE

SOB! SOB!

THAT FIGURE
OOKS FAMILIAR
HEY! I KNOW THAT GUY!
HAPPY HASEN! LONG TIME NO SEE!

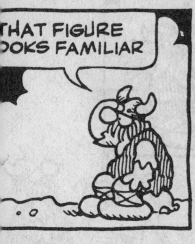

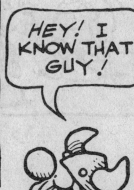

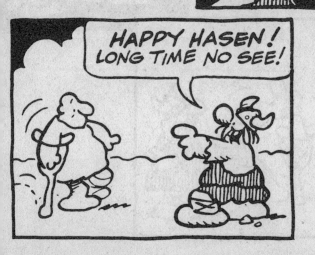

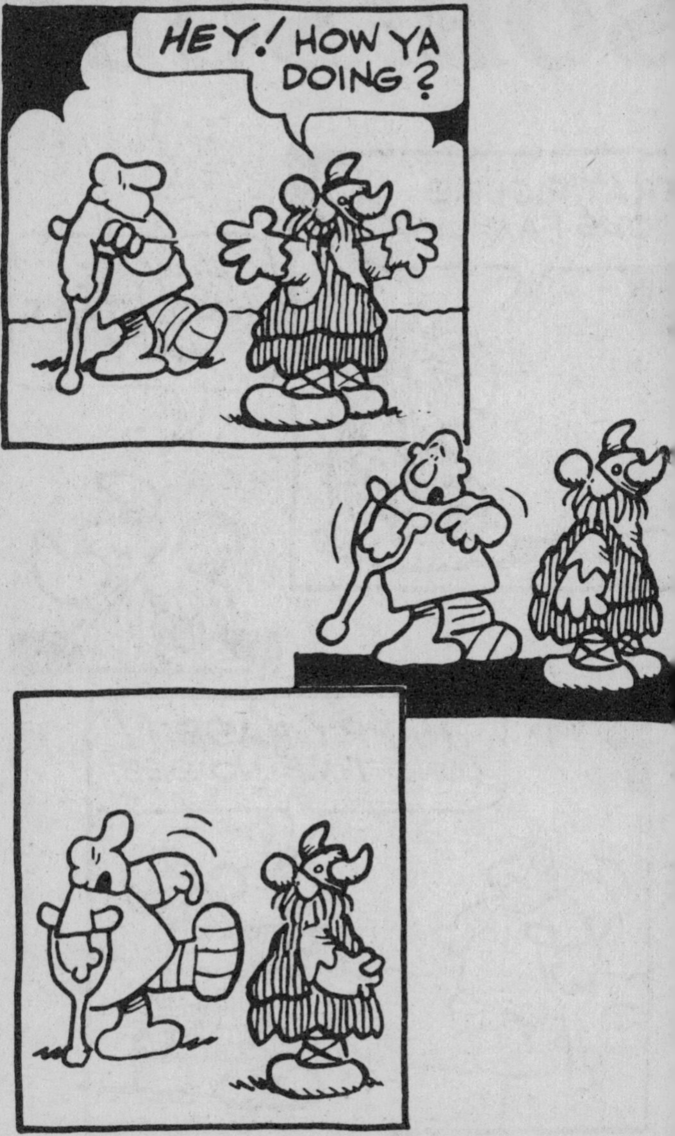
HEY! HOW YA DOING?

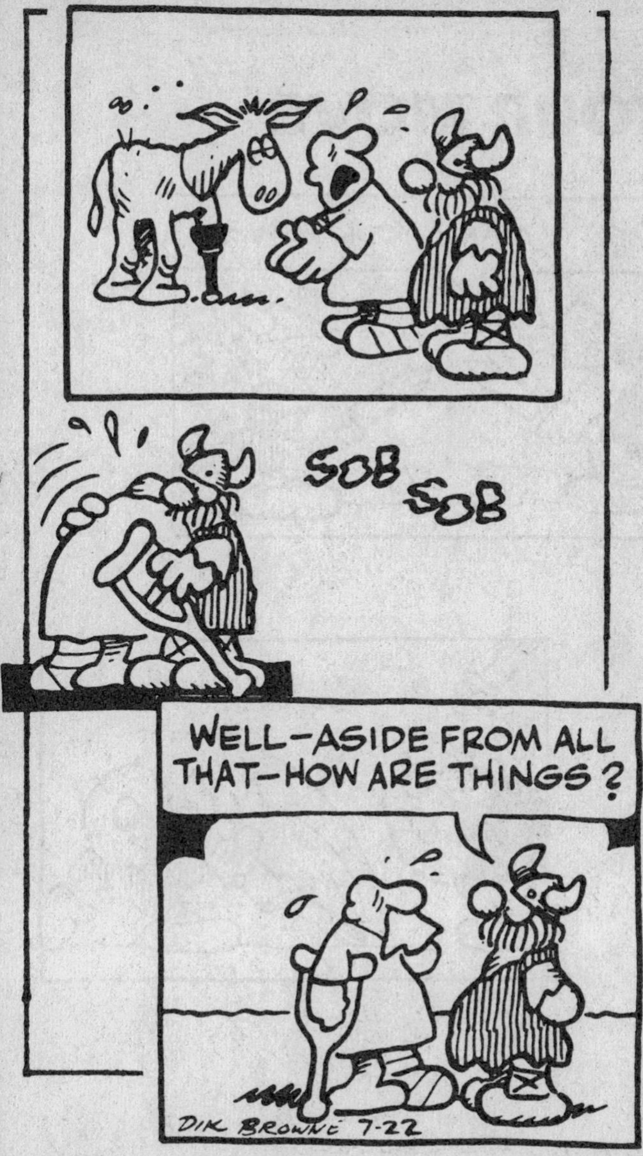
SOB SOB
WELL-ASIDE FROM ALL THAT-HOW ARE THINGS?
DIK BROWNE 7-22

YOUR MOVE

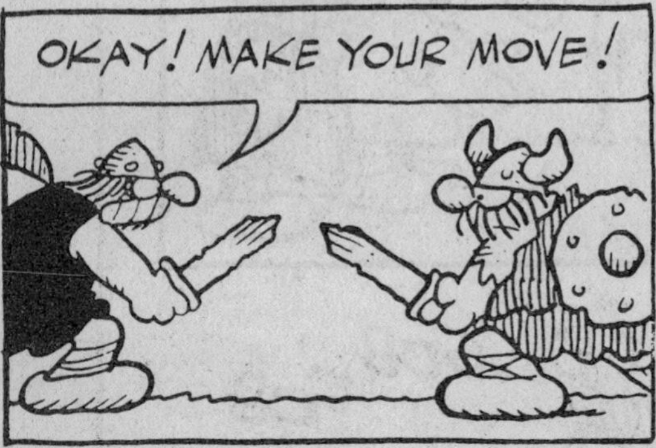
OKAY! MAKE YOUR MOVE!

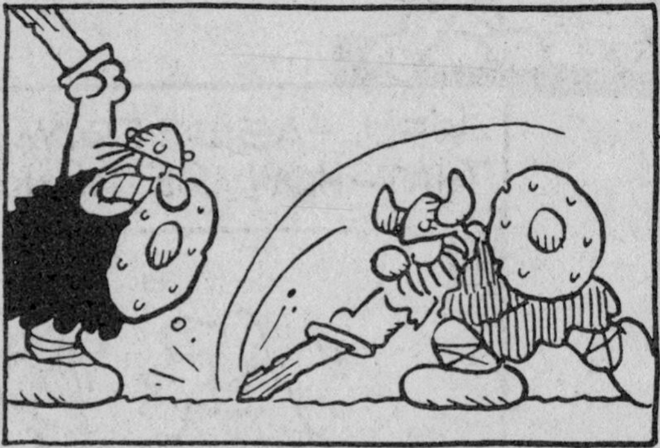

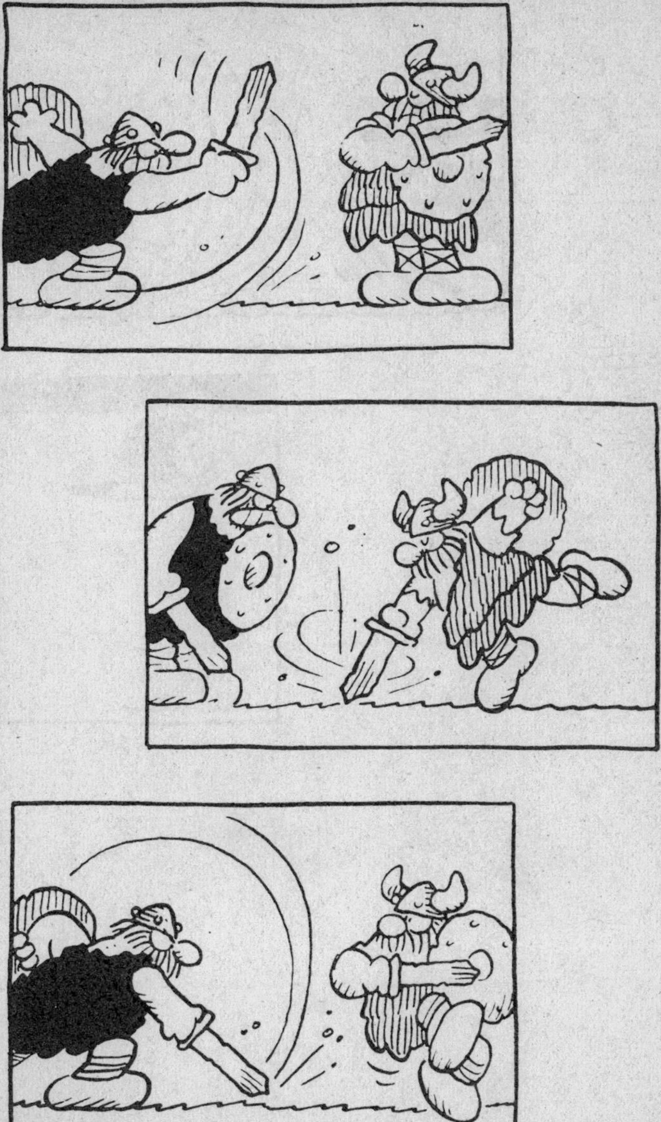

11-13

DIK BROWNE · 1983 King

HAGAR THE HORRIBLE

☐   49039-9   HAGAR #1 $1.95

☐   49045-3   HAGAR THE HORRIBLE: SACKING
PARIS ON A BUDGET $1.95

☐   49046-1   HAGAR THE HORRIBLE:
GOLDEN MAIDEN $1.95

☐   56734-X   HAGAR THE HORRIBLE: TALL TALES $1.95

☐   56739-0   HAGAR THE HORRIBLE: HEAR NO EVIL $1.95

☐   56744-7   HAGAR THE HORRIBLE: ROOM FOR
ONE MORE $1.95

☐   56749-8   HAGAR THE HORRIBLE:
HAGAR AT WORK $1.95

Buy them at your local bookstore or use this handy coupon:
Clip and mail this page with your order

TOR BOOKS—Reader Service Dept.
49 W. 24 Street, 9th Floor, New York, NY 10010

Please send me the book(s) I have checked above. I am enclosing
$_____ (please add $1.00 to cover postage and handling).
Send check or money order only—no cash or C.O.D.'s.

Mr./Mrs./Miss _____
Address _____
City _____ State/Zip _____
Please allow six weeks for delivery. Prices subject to change without
notice.

BEETLE BAILEY
THE WACKIEST G.J. IN THE ARMY

- [ ] 49003-8 BEETLE BAILEY GIANT EDITION #1 $2.50
- [ ] 49006-2 BEETLE BAILEY GIANT #2: HEY THERE! $2.50
- [ ] 49007-0 BEETLE BAILEY GIANT #3:
  ROUGH RIDERS $2.50
- [ ] 49008-9 BEETLE BAILEY GIANT #4:
  GENERAL ALERT $2.50
- [ ] 49051-8 BEETLE BAILEY GIANT #5:
  RISE AND SHINE! $2.50

- [ ] 56080-9 BEETLE BAILEY GIANT #6:
  DOUBLE TROUBLE $2.50
- [ ] 56081-7 Canada $2.95

- [ ] 56086-8 BEETLE BAILEY GIANT #7:
  YOU CRACK ME UP $2.50
- [ ] 56087-6 Canada $2.95

- [ ] 56092-2 BEETLE BAILEY GIANT #8:
  SURPRISE PACKAGE $2.50
- [ ] 56093-0 Canada $2.95

- [ ] 56098-1 BEETLE BAILEY GIANT #9:
  TOUGH LUCK $2.50
- [ ] 56099-X Canada $2.95

- [ ] 56100-7 BEETLE BAILEY #10: REVENGE $2.50
- [ ] 56101-5 Canada $2.95